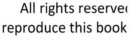
Copyright Gene E Kelly & Robert W Walker

Cover by Stephen R Walker
https://srwalkerdesigns.com/

All the characters,
incidents, and some locations are works of fiction, and
any resemblance to any persons, living, dead, or undead,
are complete coincidence

BLUE VEGAS

by Robert W. Walker

&

Gene E. Kelly

* * *

Book#1 in the Lawler Series

Acknowledgements:

From Gene E. Kelly

Thank yous. First, foremost and always, my wife Joan. For all you are and all you do. For putting up with all the various projects over the years. And everything you did to care for and mitigate the omnipresent issues that came with my immobilized, fractured arm and shoulder while working on Blue Vegas. Thank you, family and friends, for your support. Ty. Kim. Penn Jillette, for pointing me into the right head space. Mike Jones and Jennifer Szabo. Coroner's Investigators James Patrick, Warren McLeod, and Hank Missig. And consulting officers David Compson, Robert Mayer. Also, thinking of absent friends, including Chief M.E. Dr. T., Crash Investigator Phillip Scarlette, and more. Thank you, Boomer, Artist Alan White, for the Tech Wiz boost. Finally, I cannot stress enough how much Robert W. Walker's research and extensive career accomplishments in the field of police thrillers have ultimately shaped and formed this novella (soon to morph into a novella series) and Rob's having been a good friend for over twenty-five years.

— ***Gene E. Kelly, March 2024, Las Vegas, Nevada.***

Brief author bio on Gene E. Kelly at end of Blue Vegas

From Robert W. Walker

*My undying gratitude to my wife, Miranda Phillips Walker, for having literally saved my life more than once, being an observant and skilled registered nurse, thus allowing me the opportunity to carry on with my writing career as well as enjoy a longer life! And for her caring for me during recovery. Secondly, my children, step-ones and grand ones, as well as my son, Stephen, who has been so very patient and helpful every step of the way in assisting with the technical difficulty hurdles that Gene and I faced in the creation of **BLUE VEGAS**. For extensive editing help, I must thank my wonderful editors Diane Harrison of Canada, my #1 fan and a great heart of gold; secondly, my wonderful narrator and editor on my audiobooks, Tom Fria, who is my go-to guy for quick fixes. Finally, I must also thank our dog Scout, who had alerted on me while I had fallen unconscious with brain hemorrhaging via a stroke. Scout did the famous Lassie thing and got help. And oh yes, not to forget; without the diligence and knowledge of Officer Gene E. Kelly, this novella series could not have been conceived and nourished this far and with plans for more.*

**–- Robert W. Walker, March 2024,
Nitro, West Virginia.**

Brief author bio - *Robert W. Walker at end of book one
Blue Vegas*

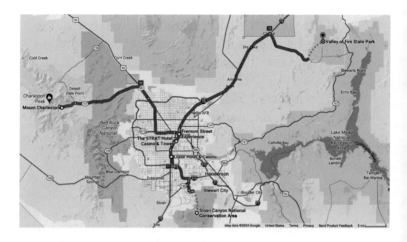

ONE

Code 411-11: careful what you say aloud over police radio.

Las Vegas NV, CCCO Clark County Coroner's Office Morgue: Investigators' Night Class

"In a moment, *classss*, we'll be heading back to *intake*, began Dr. Jessica Coran, newly retired FBI forensics expert and medical examiner. Coran had stepped away from her FBI career and was now a master instructor for Las Vegas' Clark County Coroner's Investigation Academy. She'd gotten into the habit of exaggerating the word class as *classss* and curtailing the epitaph God damn for her adult students in thumbnail fashion, as a quick, seemingly less offensive *g'damn*.

1

One of the younger student applicants from one of the small non-Las Vegas Metro departments whispered in Joe Lawler's ear, "*Intake, intake?*"

"Lawler whispered back, "Examination room, you know, autopsy, the cooler, decomp, all that."

"Decomp?"

"Decomposition cooler."

M.E. Coran asked Lawler if he'd care to take over her class. When he declined, she continued, saying, "Now, as part of your first night's orientation at the Las Vegas, Clark County's *Coroner Investigator Academy*, glove up!" The Academy Director and Chief Coroner's Investigator passed around three tissue-sized boxes, each filled with blue latex gloves, in small, medium, and extra-large. "Take two, glove up!" Dr. Jessica Coran repeated, adding, "And remove your ties, or anything that might touch, spill, fall or flop out and onto the body of the deceased during your examinations."

"You mean like a Junior Mint?" joked a tall, thin, over-the-hill fellow named Fred.

"*Our* examinations?" asked another young officer, a recent graduate of the police academy, who'd put this required class off. His question got him a stare-down and a quick glance at Coran's student list. She had a mugshot beside each name.

The well-tested, experienced medical examiner ignored the question and led her class from the room and down the hallway where the 'deep' Dungeons & Dragons *autopsy room* awaited. Where the grim 'teachable moments' in the medical profession were passed on to the naïve officers, who'd given little thought to their training duties after graduation from the police academy.

The passage to the horror *classss* had Joe Lawler steeling himself, no matter that he'd gone through this kind of training in Fox Lake County, Illinois and Cook County, Chicago, years before. *Still, death and autopsy training*, Lawler mentally likened to recovering bodies in a blackwater river. *Not even the most experienced diver was ever fully ready for a bloated white face shooting out of the darkness straight for a guy's face mask.*

Lawler's present thoughts, however, were on his new chief, Chief of the City of Stewart PD, Gabe Lewis. Although Lawler only held a part-time status at Stewart PD, the chief had imparted in his flat out, no-nonsense, no-humanity tone, "Any *additional part-time work* taken on by one of *my* investigators or my LEO peace officers must be pre-approved by me! I mean it's fine up to a point!" The chief was howling this for anyone in the station, but it was really meant for Joe Lawler–as he'd taken on extra hours in Las Vegas.

This meant, Stewart Police detail came first and foremost, even if a man lost his other job. It was all at the chief's discretion, that any outside job may or may not *interfere* with Joe's Stewart Police duties, and that Stewart PD had first dibs on Joe's work schedule, despite the fact that Joe only held a part-time badge with Stewart.

3

"Pure bullshit," he muttered, thinking it was only to himself until Dr. Coran assured him that, "This training–even for an old dog like you, Lawler, saves time for the coroner's office to concentrate on actual murder as opposed to overdoses and suicides."

"Sorry, doc…didn't mean it that way."

"How else do you use bullshit?" she half-joked, getting smirks from the others as the elevator went down to a quiet hum.

Lawler returned to his nagging thought: While the Stewart Departmental Police manual did indeed say that if an officer is engaged in other work, such as a security guard at a casino or corporation, that primary duties, full or part-time as a police officer in Stewart meant that Stewart came first. Lawler'd held a part-time badge with the city for over six months now. Any other part-time position Joe held would have the same hold on his time as did the town of Stewart. First come, first served, assigned, and negotiated when the monthly schedule was announced. He understood based on the schedule that any full-time position would have priority choice on an officer's hours, but part-time? And Chief Lewis *needn't've* shouted this for the squad room to then buzz about.

The Stewart City Manual also had many an archaic rule as well. Such as a mandatory residence proximity to the department, and a dumb requirement to have a phone landline, in addition to any cellular phones owned or assigned. No one had a landline anymore. But Chief 'Asshole' Lewis said, "I expect *all* officers to follow *all* rules and *all* regulations outlined in the Stewart Police manual."

During the crowded elevator ride and the walk through the tunnel of grimness: bland white walls to the autopsy room, Lawler had pulled and snapped on his latex gloves with practiced ease. In fact, having an idea what was coming, he *double* gloved. This while some in the class tore their gloves while struggling to put them on. Many had to start over. Joe glanced at the single female in the class, a good-looking blonde, blue eyed young woman that he only knew as Loudin. The 'blue knight' in him wanted to give her a lesson on glove comportment, but when she noticed his attention, he quickly dropped the hero notion, nodding instead, pretending to concentrate on Coran's Academy syllabus in his blue-gloved hand.

"Those of you who graduate from this endgame of the academy, you will be full Coroner Investigators, with duties and responsibilities as outlined and enumerated in County Code... code *ahh* hell, I forget, let's call it *XYZ* for purposes of *now*..."

TWO

Code 10-1: bad radio signal

"Follow me back." Dr. Coran said, leading the way.

Lawler had never seen such a clean and brightly lit Coroner's Morgue. From the front lobby, and back to the front administrative offices and cubicles, there was no smell of chemicals, disinfectant, or decomposing human bodies. The Academy classroom was between the front offices and the morgue. You could smell some decomposition whenever someone walked through the door back toward the morgue. But only now, as the class walked down the hallway, past different examination, X-ray and file rooms, the odor became more distinct, and stronger and stronger.

Professor Coran paused just outside the double doors with the windowed portholes at eye level. "Most of you have some experience with scenes of death already. Some of you do not. If you do feel dizzy or ill, sit down on the floor. We don't want anyone falling and splitting their head open on our tile floor. If you do need to vomit, please just grab one of the plastic lined waste baskets next to every gurney."

Lawler stood close, near the front, peeking through the windows, still awed, as he'd never seen such a clean morgue. Coran pushed open the doors, and everyone filed inside, silent. They were hit by the distinct odor of human decay, and some decomposition, *but nothing like the morgues in Illinois*, he was thinking. The Lake County morgue was terrible, with evidence rooms and closets, shelves, sinks, metal gurneys, with old decomp and fluids that built up over time recalled images of layers of ice on an Illinois highway. No matter how much the scut work attendants scrubbed and disinfected, that odor seeped in and built up over the long years. But this was nothing compared to the Cook County Morgue in Chicago. That was still likely a completely disgusting mess.

In addition to the lack of the worst smells, Lawler noted how pristine and clean this facility was. Of course, there was no dim mood lighting that the public saw on television, but the stainless- steel sinks, clean white painted shelves and cabinets, with bright red tile backsplash, along with bright and clean large red and white tiled flooring. The place almost said, 'home kitchen'. The whole ambience was a brightly lit surprise, a room with ample fluorescents overhead and under cabinets, as well as hinged multi directional incandescent lamps aimed at exam points.

Each of the decedent's remains lay on a tan plastic rolling gurney, with a hole in the end, and slight tilt designed to facilitate the drainage of human fluids, water, waste, and cleaning products.

"Most of these decedents will be discharged from the office in a day. Three days at the most, unless there is some reason to hold them longer. When one of the students asked about the fast turnaround time, Dr. Coran replied, "Coroner Telgenhoff aka Dr. T insists and prides himself on a quick professional examination and turnaround time. Still, some more complicated court cases, and unidentified John Does are kept back in the decomp cooler, within the cooler. There are no individual drawers with bodies. Too many moving parts, slides, wheels and crevices to clean. Unless they are going to be here awhile, then they come in, then placed on a plastic gurney that is easily hosed down and washes speedily and so, the corpse is discharged out to the NOK's chosen funeral homes."

"Next of kin," Kathi Loudin told a younger female, Joe liking her whiskey voice.

"Yeah, NOK," Lawler unnecessarily added.

Loudin nodded as if to say thanks, while Coran gave Joe the stare.

Without warning, Dr. Coran yanked away the sheet from a middle-aged male Caucasian. Balding. Some burgundy and purple lividity pooled in concentric blobs a couple inches apart where he lay face up on his gurney. There was some purge from his nose, and clear pus like excretion seeping from each corner of his mouth.

THREE

10-2: safe status.

M.E. Jessica Coran spoke as she performed a full body examination of the deceased, whose toe tag marked him as John *East-Tunnel* Doe. A dozen or so John and Jane Does have been listed on the briefing room white board, "A good thing for our classes, not so good for the deceased," Coran quietly noted. "True at any given time. All investigators are expected to work on identifying these *ahhh*, lost souls, as time allows. To notify their next of kin as soon as possible. That is during your regular work week. Middle names, such as *East-Tunnel* here are assigned to each case based on where the corpse was found, you know, to differentiate each case, along with the case number of course. Mr. John *East-Tunnel* Doe here, he was brought in this morning. Was part of the many communities of homeless, unhoused, underground tunnel-dwellers that set up homes and living areas in the graffiti-filled, cement drainage washes under the streets of Las Vegas."

"East-Tunnel," said Loudin. "I get it. He had no *other* identifying info on his person other than location."

"Often the case with the homeless, yes," replied the professor.

"Could've called him 'Drain Doe," added Fred. "The Tunnels are called drains by the locals."

Coran didn't even give Fred a half smirk, but rather went to providing the class with her physical example of what they would be expected to do in the field when called to a death scene. She began with Mr. *Drain* Doe's feet, examining the dirty toes, cracked nails, and between toes, and up the ankles, calves, behind the knees. She touched and palpated the skin and muscles, tendons, bending and twisting on joints, looking for breaks, cuts, bruises, needle marks, or crepitus."

"What is it, Fred?" she asked as the thin man's hand rose.

"What is *crap-itus*?" he asked with a pinched expression.

"Crep-itus," she corrected. "Bone cracking sound when the neck, in particular, is moved, but also in other joints. Usually just air bubbles in you and me—the living, but signs of injury in the dead. Students, we're talking now of anything that doesn't come as *stock* issue on a human body, anything that *may* provide information and clues about the cause and manner of death. We're not expecting you to delve into any orifices or to dissect or learn the art of the Stryker saw."

She then began sneezing into her surgical mask and pulled the mask down for a large handkerchief instead. She blew her nose into the hanky.

Coran regained herself. "You need to follow a routine, doing the same full body examination on every death call you respond to. If you develop a *habitual* way to perform a proper exam, then you're far less likely to accidentally overlook or miss something in the field."

Dr. Coran went on with a deft hand, completing a thorough head-to-toe examination. She opened the man's eyes and directed her students to note there was no sign of dark spots or petechiae on the eyes, which would be indicative of suffocation or strangulation. "Check in his mouth, behind his ears, between his fingers and toes. Everywhere on his body from top to bottom, yes, literally speaking—or if you like, head-to-toe, or from toes to head."

Coran then directed the two closest adults in the adult class, one of which was Lawler, to roll and hold Mr. Doe on his side. "You'll probably be by yourself in the field. If you can roll and hold him, great. Otherwise carefully roll the deceased or lift his shoulders and legs individually to perform your exam. Just don't skip any part of a thorough in *situ* exam for your *medico-legal* investigation."

"It is unlawful for anyone, not the family, nor the public, not even Crime Scene Analysts/Investigators, or Police Officers to touch, move, or interfere with a decedent until *you* have determined time of death, and *you* have performed *your* full examination and initial report, and only then do you release the body and scene of death to the family, or to the funeral home on notation to transport to their facility, or back to the Clark County Las Vegas Coroner's Office as *you* alone direct."

"No sheets or other cover may go on the corpse until you release it. No chalk outlines. These can leave contaminates and destroy trace evidence on the body. Again, no chalk outlines. That is just in the movies and BF."

11

"Best Friend?" asked a confused Loudin.

"Coran gave her the cold stare and said, "Before Forensics, or, I should say Before TV Forensics. Used to be you'd come on a scene, well and good, and there'd be the chalk outline. Used to say to the police, "I see the chalk fairy has been here, but thankfully, almost never happens anymore."

Coran watched carefully as each student took a turn trying to do a textbook style, full-body, hands on exam of each of the bodies. She watched to see if anyone had any particular aversion or squeamishness, or any other quirk that might need remedial work or help.

When it was Lawler's turn, he tried to do it as Coran had demonstrated. When he was manipulating the elbow, then checking the hands and wrist for crepitus, he was suddenly taken back to when he was a rookie cop in Morainal Hills, Illinois, a burb of Chicago, and first shook hands with a corpse. And not metaphorically.

Coran had efficiently and methodically finished with John *East-Tunnel* Doe. She'd moved onto a "...fresh' corpse, a Jane Doe, an attractive, blonde Caucasian professional dancer in her mid-thirties with large breast implants, and a number of obvious piercings, the small holes where the on-scene investigator had removed rings and jewelry."

With the second *g'damn* examination over with, this of the Jane Doe, Coran went to what she called, "An honest conundrum, a messy challenge for the books, a puzzle of injuries to a Black man. It's a weird bicyclist versus truck, traffic death. Guess who was on the bike…"

Coran proved an excellent teacher and quickly moved onto an overweight Hispanic airplane pilot whose private plane had crashed two days before. His body charred, torn. and laced with multi-colored rubber insulation-covered electrical wire, making him a cyborg. The wires and terminal caps embedded and woven through his entire body not even the eldest student, Joe Lawler had ever seen in a career's worth of automotive accidents. Never anything like this.

"This one's identified from papers found in the plane's glove compartment, so he's a Juan Garcia, family notified, but in this condition, I'll need more time than we have here tonight, so…but honestly, I don't want any family seeing him *as is*."

"In the cooler?" said Lawler, unhesitatingly covering Juan and taking him to the cooler, a spacious big room where the icy cold had Joe wanting to rush in and out. No wall compartments. *Cool*, he thought.

"Not sure if we have time for *Cement Sarcophagus* guy either," she told the class while glancing at her watch, the one gifted to her upon her retirement from the FBI.

"Huge man," commented Loudin, a half-smile creasing her lips.

"Too big, and given the extra weight of the cement, too heavy for any wheeled gurney. It's why he's the only one on a stainless-steel, heavy-duty table. There're

13

portions of stone mixed concrete crumbling inward about the head, desert dirt, and still living spiders climbing in and out of the forehead bullet hole. Cause of death fairly certain in John *Desert* Doe's case—we also get a lot of his *Desert* relatives here."

This was the only corpse that Lawler had to turn away from, and his action was not unmissed by Coran. "You okay, Joe?" she asked.

"Yeah, just picturing the people who could bury a man in concrete like this; pictured Vincent Price and Peter Lorie out in the desert doing it, like in their horror films."

"Might want to use Robert De Niro and Joe Pesci for this business, Joe." Coran waved a finger at Lawler, a sign that she wanted to go on, but she then said, "I've been told the mob's been kicked out of Vegas by the politicians working with the big corporations. Was I told wrong?"

"I've been told the same," replied Joe. "But no amount of politics or big money can eradicate all evil anywhere, now can it? In fact, it's often the case they all wrap 'round one'nuther like snakes in a pit.'"

Fred cleared his throat and said in his best assuring tone, "For the most part, Dr. Coran, you were told right. The casinos are run by the hotel owners nowadays—biggest of them for sure."

Dr. Coran had, with her assistant's help, made the row of bare feet with toe tags sticking from white sheets on wheeled gurneys disappear. Lawler and the other students had seen the big toes of men, the petite toes of women, indeterminate toes, and one an obvious child's tagged toe. The little one appeared perhaps seven or eight years of age. Obvious to Lawler that Dr. Coran had decided to hold the child back for another day, or rather night.

In the decomp cooler, when he'd returned Cyborg Man there, Lawler had nosily looked about, seeing a score of bodies that Dr. Coran, no doubt, held back for other upcoming night classes. Then he considered another thought. *Had she selected the most unusual and odd cases for the benefit of a cop who'd seen it all—him? Maybe, maybe not.* Whatever her reasons, she'd managed to get a number of little green buckets filled with her students' combined vomit.

A score of bodies, which is less than most morgues maintain at any given time, at least in Illinois, he thought. Most of the bodies were kept inside the cooler room, out of sight and near but not completely frozen meant no goopy excretions. The cooler room had a small back room as well for various tagged body parts, and evidentiary pieces of human anatomy, while some smaller pieces of human flesh floated in tightly sealed fluid bottles of alcohol or formaldehyde.

He was still rubbernecking as he pushed Cyborg man, trying to slide the gurney between two cadavers parked against the back wall. In so doing, he accidentally bumped one of the gurneys hard enough that the decedent's right arm fell from beneath the sheet, now dangling at the gurney's edge. Joe cursed and took the cold, raw meat like hand into his own to return it below the sheet. It made him recall a time in Illinois, when he was still a rookie street cop in training, when he had been set up to shake hands with a fresh corpse. Setup by a prankster cop named Boone who was affectionately called Boomer.

Lawler even recalled the good old Illinois 10 code call number for such a case:
10-67 - Report of death. Morainal Hills IL, 921 Mulberry Street: MHPD swing shift 8:44 pm.

Early in his work as a newly minted patrol officer in one Chicago suburban county, Lawler was assigned a one-week ride along with a veteran of Morainal Hills PD, Steve Boone, '*The Boomer*'. This short ride that Lawler thought back to had been primarily an orientation and to learn local streets there in Morainal and Department SOP. At the time, Joe found himself on solo patrol in a navy blue unmarked chevy squad car of his own. Although this was his first full-time municipal street cop job, with health insurance and benefits, he'd had a few years' experience working other part-time LEO jobs, as a County Sheriff's boat patrol Officer, County Forest Preserve Ranger-Police, and had had a part-time weekend badge writing traffic tickets for a one-horse town on the Wisconsin border that intersected with two major highways. Although Lawler was treated very much like a rookie to the Morainal Hills area, he was still expected to pull his weight and work his own car, shifts, and calls, and this was almost immediately. Just the same, other officers on his shift were often dispatched, or tagged along to *shadow* him.

Morainal Hills was a town with a unique and diverse geography, from the flatwoods and prairie fields of Northern Illinois, in that there were low rolling glacial hills, and a series of canals and lakes that had drawn summer tourists out of Chicago for their boating and beach needs, not to mention the evening dance hall recreations. This all during the 1940s and '50s. There were slot machines and booze during prohibition. A number of small, wooded neighborhoods with cape cod summer vacation houses filled the area like camp cabins built back then.

While far from the normal sense of a rookie, Lawler accepted the fact that in the eyes of the brass and the beat cops, he was new here, so he was just another 'rookie'. Certainly, he was being treated as a rookie to Vegas ways, and so it was generally directed and accepted that Officer Lawler would simply respond to every call that the new guy was available for, and some that were in adjacent sister towns and municipalities. He had to admit, it did prove a great way to *power-add* training and experience. This routine did give the staff and senior officers an opportunity to see how he might react under pressure and in a variety of calls and situations. Expected, he realized, specially while on the standard twelve-month probation period.

MHPD Senior Officer Boone had once texted Lawler, ordering him to meet Boone a few blocks from a *man down,* likely a natural death call. Boone locked up his own marked patrol car and hopped into the passenger seat of Lawler's unmarked cruiser. Boone didn't hesitate to push Lawler's ditty bag, metal K-Light and gear into a pile on the floorboard to make room.

17

On the way, Boone told him that although Boone'd caught the call and was going to be the reporting officer, so he expected Lawler to *run* the call, and to do all the paperwork on scene and afterward back at *the barn*.

Lawler recalled having cracked his window, enjoying the cool of early fall, the cool against his cheek, ignoring Boone's order to close 'the damn window'. But Joe's attention to a half moonlit Illinois sky above was replaced when he saw a herd of cop cars ahead. He felt only somewhat surprised to see more than a few patrol cars outside their zones, these alongside squad cars from a couple of neighboring towns, all nestled in the street and a short gravel driveway. Even Morainal Village and Morainal Woods Cops had drifted this way.

"What's going on, Boone? Why the crowd?" Lawler remembered asking.

"Not a whole lot going on tonight," Boone had said, adding, "not nuff in their own patch. Least not enough for these jokers, so when there's an interesting call, well… b'sides, they *wanna* meet the new guy in town– you! Take your measure, watch ya work, be social, and even lend a hand and spit out their helpful advice. Hell, you'll need it to navigate *our* area. new procedures and surrounding areas new to your *ahh*, experience."

Lawler recalled having frowned at this and having imagined how nice it'd be to go sit on a beach somewhere, but not with Boomer. It felt like he was being pimped with Boone's work, and maybe more, but he let it go. With Boone ahead of him, and the two of them big, stout men, they'd easily parted the others as they'd walked through the crowd of blue and brown uniformed men and women.

Surveying the outside and then the inside, Lawler recalled how simple it'd been to sum the place up. The home was typical of many local neighborhoods, both in and around Chicago and now in the Vegas area. But the Chicago northern burbs had lakes, so of course, a series of identical small Cape Cod design houses, built as summer vacation homes in the woods by the lakes. Two bedrooms, combo living and dining room, and a very tight galley kitchen. One bathroom. Often with one gas heater in the living room, with no room to room heat ducts. No AC.

As Joe remembered it, inside the home, he and Boone found the place moderately clean, but dishes in the sink, a pile of dirty shoes by the front door, and some clothes on the floor in the short hallway to bedrooms and bath. The home had the kind of scratched wood and plaid furniture cheaply gotten from an outlet store. The cramped space smelled of cigarettes, and moving closer to the bathroom, the unmistakable smell of an unflushed toilet had assailed the senses.

Bathrooms in such quickly built homes were of the small efficiency sort, just enough room for a tub hiding behind a shower curtain, a toilet, and a small single pedestal sink with a used bar of soap perched on the back, along with a mirrored medicine cabinet on the wall above. Eerily the mirror stood pulled open at just the right angle as to reflect Joe's image, capturing him like a sudden still photo. Damn mirrors under these circumstances always found Lawler in more cases than he'd care to remember now. It was as if the mirror always asked, *Just who is this curious intruder?*

Then would come the awful sight of a bruised and naked, gray-haired old fella's arm snaking out at the elbow, the arm caught between the mostly closed door and a door jam. That night with Boone, the arm protruded from a barely open and haphazardly painted white wooden door with equally chipped and dry splotches of errant paint.

Lawler had eventually come to the realization that he wasn't the only rookie that night being tested, as the training officer from a southeast bordering town had brought his trainee along. After having his image caught by the oddly pointed mirror, Lawler had walked down the short hallway. He'd wanted a moment to brace himself. Then behind him there stood Boone and others, and they appeared at war with the bathroom door, three cops pushing and pulling but not too much force used, being somewhat gentle as they took turns cursing, trying to get the bathroom door open without damaging the crime scene or decedent. But every time they pushed, and released, the body weight, likely fallen and wedged between the tub and door, would push back: *a dead man pushing back, shutting the door against the intruders.* Lawler'd had the eerie feeling that the old man was even in death pushing back against the door, not just from the other side of the door, but from the other side of death, trying to stay, crying out, "Hell no, I won't go!"

Boomer broke the silence, saying, "Officer Smith, Officer Lawler, I'd like you to meet our friend on the floor, Mr. Burkhoelter. To get to the deceased's hand, Boone had dropped to his knees, and then he'd given the decedent a hearty handshake, and grabbed officer Smith's wrist and pushed his palm against the dead man's palm. Smith recoiled in horror and tripped backward, ending his back-peddle against a hallway wall, knocking a couple of family photos off their nails, breaking one glass frame.

No one laughed at him. But all eyes turned to the other new guy as Boone held the dead man's hand out to Joe, who worried that he might appear to be hesitant and thinking too long, as the proverbial clock was ticking, and the others were all expectantly watching Lawler.

Lawler considered the possibility of destroying evidence on what was likely a *natural-causes-died-on-commode-case, the fact that the family was next door, and "nobody here but us cops," and the possibility of disease in that then HIV era.* Regardless of it all, he reached out, took the decedent's hand from Boone, and gave it a strong pump or two, just to appear one of the tough guys.

"Hello Mr. Burkhoelter," Lawler began while pumping the dead man's cold paw. "I'm sorry to be meeting you under these circumstances, but rest assured, we will do our best for you and your family. Please let me know if there's anything we can do to make your transitional time from this mortal coil any easier."

No one belly laughed, but there were some smirks and chuckles. Lawler felt quite sure this smoothed the road to acceptance into the loose and rocky fraternity of

LEOs. Although nowadays, the blue line of solidarity was starting to seriously blur and break.

***

Disposition Code S, End of class. Out of the cold. Las Vegas NV CCCO Morgue, Autopsy Room. 12:20 am.

When Lawler came back to the here and now, and into the autopsy exam room from the cooler, he saw that only old guy veteran Fred, sweet-looking Loudin, a few others he did not yet know, and Lawler himself, had held back from puking in the green buckets. All the others had, to one degree or another, spit up. But fortunately, no one had so loudly vomited that *puking* had become contagious among the night class. Professor Coran had them rinse their own buckets down the sink drains, using the ample disinfectant cleaners to restore the area to its pristine pre-class state.

Had Dr. Coran selected the most unusual cases a cops who'd seen it all—he and Fred perhaps? Maybe, maybe not. Whatever her reasons, she'd managed to get more than several little green buckets filled with her students' combined vomit.

FOUR

999—Cop only share for Deja'vu; not official code.

Stewart NV, SPD, 6:20 pm on the 5:00 pm - 5:00 am power shift.

Early in his work as a new but retread patrol officer in the neon adult circus called Las Vegas, Joseph Lawler, despite his long career in law enforcement, knew on moving here that he'd be treated like a rookie. He'd left a job as a Police Captain in the small midwestern town of Morainal Hills, a far north burb of Chicago. He'd made the move, fed up with the politics that'd strangled him at the job there. He did so with a combined six years as an experienced US Marine JAG Sergeant, County Boat Patrol Officer, Beat Cop, a Park and Boat Patrol officer, and a County Forest Preserve Ranger. So, after one week of riding along and being shown the streets of *this* most unusual Glitter Town that he now found himself in, he was assigned a non-descript, tarnished brown, unmarked patrol car of his own and told to, "Go enforce traffic and answer calls on the 5:30 pm to 05:30 am overnight shift." Chief Lewis' first orders sounded so expected that they almost turned Joe's stomach with a cache of bad memories involving administrators like this man.

The prowl car assigned to him from the Stewart PD's carpool was a well-used, nondescript brown sedan with a horrible noise inside the cab whenever cranked and moving. It took Lawler some time to understand the cause of the strange noise; it proved to be the front dashboard, which rattled badly from being terribly loose from its moorings. He immediately christened his ride 'The Rattler' and tried his damn best to ignore the irritating, nerve-biting rattle.

Being still very much a rookie to Vegas ways, it was generally directed and accepted that Officer Lawler might simply respond to every call in every town in and around Stewart, and in Vegas itself when practical; that the new guy was available to stand by and assist. That he be prepared for cleanup duty in adjacent sister towns and municipalities as well. All determined as a good way to power-add training and experience.

During Lawler's orientation and ride along with another officer, he was dispatched along with Officer Mick the Trick" Finnegan. Soon enough, the pair were ordered to a death investigation at a private residence in the Old Town section of Stewart. Old Town was a neighborhood that'd once been a new development of little 700 square foot square shaped cottage homes built in the 1930s for people flooding into the city to find work on the Dam. Spare homes, each an identical box, each with a small eat-in kitchen adjacent and open to a small living room, and a closet sized hallway that led to a bathroom, and a separate bedroom door or two. Nowadays they were often *tricked out* with room additions, attic dormers, and identical tan stucco siding as year-round family homes, similarly to the Cape Cod vacation homes Joe knew from the Midwest. *Some* of the Stewart yards, though tiny by Midwest standards, boasted full lawns and lush landscaping. This was despite years of education, proffered bribes in the form of homeowner subsidies, irrigation law enforcement, and threats by the Nevada Water Authority.

Lawler cracked his window, enjoying the cool of early fall, the cool against his cheek, ignoring Mick's order to 'close the damn window', sounding like good old Boomer, who he'd left to the past or thought so.

Lawler felt only somewhat surprised to see more than a few patrol cars and SUVs from SPD and neighboring police agencies parked near the call location. There was a Vegas Marshall, Henderson and Boulder City PDs, and even a gal from BLM, Bureau of Land Management enforcement. They'd all sneaked across their borders to take a peek at Lawler's personality and demeanor. Not one from Vegas Metro though.

"What's going on, Mick? Multi-jurisdiction homicides? Joe asked, knowing the answer.

"There's a very rare, shared lull in the action in our fair valley for the moment," began the short, stocky Mick, "and I suspect they *wanna* lay eyeballs on the new guy in town–you!"

"You been bragging on getting to ride with me, Mick?" Joe, knowing what Mick was going to add, finished for Finnegan, saying, "Take my measure, watch *me* work, be sociable, and even lend a hand as they give me *helpful* advice. Hell, I'll need all the help and advice I can get to navigate Vegas procedures and surrounding areas like Henderson and Stewart, places new to me, sure, I get it…"

Before Lawler might continue, before he even had the vehicle fully in park, Mick had already leapt from the car and was headed up the paver walkway, through the gravel, cacti and Joshua scrub desert-scaped yard toward the wide-open front door.

Lawler, by comparison, eased from the 'Rattler. A tall, stout man, Lawler strode easily past a couple of Cops smoking outside the door. Each offered companionable nods. Then through the living room and back into the bathroom, where BLM and the Marshall were already sniffing around the CCCO Coroner's Investigator. She was a short red head in tailored green suit and slacks, with a laminate ID clipped to her pocket and a gold seven-point CCCO Investigator's badge on her belt. She also had a curvy model's figure and a clipboard. *Cops*, he thought, *so much in common no matter the state.*

She paused from counting prescription bottles and pills from the medicine cabinet long enough to offer Joe her gloved hand. "Your Lawler, right? I'm Perkins. I saw you back at the Coroner's Office the other night." They shook hands.

"Nice to meet you," Lawler replied.

Handing him her clipboard, she said, "You're late. Do me a solid and sign the forms on the dotted lines."

Lawler wasn't late, but he took the clipboard and looked over the pages. The forms were a bit different than those he was used to, but it looked like pretty standard, preliminary stuff. He signed.

Mick called from the bedroom. "Hey Joe! Come on back here a minute!"

"Do you mind?" he caught himself asking her.

"No, go ahead. Take a look." She waved at the Marshall and the BLM gal. "They'll keep me company until you get back."

Joe had found the home moderately clean, but with dishes and a variety of liquor bottles in the sink, and piles of dirty clothes strewn about from bathroom to bedroom. The home décor appeared to've come from the cheapest of box stores and played well to the odors permeating the place. Cigars and votive candles? The candles maybe meant to fend off the cigar smell, maybe? Walking deeper in toward the bedroom, a familiar, unmistakable odor of urine and feces. It all looked eerily similar to hundreds of calls he'd been on in his long career.

Lawler walked in and immediately saw the trouble. Mick nodded as if he expected an autoerotic death, but how'd he gotten such a notion from the dispatcher's words, Joe could not square up. Joe saw the source of the repugnant odor—urine and feces on the decedent's purple paisley board shorts. Mick stared at Joe. "We oughta be able to get the poor bastard down, but protocol says we can't…fuckin' regs." Joe contemplated the suicide victim and how the man'd hung himself either intentionally or not intending to take it so far as a "Dead end," as Mick now put it. *Summabitch…*" Mick sounded tired. He likely wanted someone else to do the work here so he could go home, and Joe understood that desire, as he felt it himself.

Mick said hello to the dead man, and then said, "Officer Lawler, I'd like you to meet my good buddy on the damn door, hanging around, you might say, *Mr. Campanella.* Mick reared back as if to give the decedent's hand a hearty high-five. Then he held the gray hand up for Joe, expecting Lawler, before others, to meet the dead man's palm with his own.

Joe nervously looked around, taking in the scene while waiting for CCCO Investigator Perkins to signal the next step. When she was done, she released the body to the on-call funeral home drivers for transport to the Coroner's Office—Then the Stewart Police's job on this one would begin in earnest.

Joe'd been through this scenario before. Actually, a high-five was easy compared to a full-on handshake with the dead. But he remembered what Dr. Coran had said in the Investigator's class, about no one touching the body or scene of death until directed or released by the Coroner's Investigator—and he snatched Mick's hand by the wrist before he could connect with the decedent's palm.

"Are you F'in crazy Mick? Trying to get me fired at the Coroner's Office before I even start? I need the full-time pay and health benefits you selfish bastard!"

"*Heyyy,* just tryin' to lighten the moment, pal." Mick was abashed and although he wouldn't show it, a little hurt. "I wasn't actually going to do it," he lied, not knowing how far he could trust the new guy.

State to state, some things about this work simply proved *the job*'s *the job*, no matter what the borders or jurisdictions might be. Just as with Boone's shenanigans in Illinois, here was Mick after the same release of fear and loathing as Boone had sought thousands of miles away. In fact, the coroner for Vegas proper, Dr. T as everyone called Telgenhoff, could and would have an officer's badge if he should learn of any 'hand-holding' or other disrespect toward or touching of the deceased before proper protocol was followed, meaning hands-off until *he,* or one of his trained men, took the photos and did the initial exam—what Lawler was training for under Dr. Coran's watchful eye. This answered another reason that Boomer in Illinois and Mick the Trick in Vegas played these 'dangerous' games. To get away with breaking rules and regs that had gotten so complicated and so many that they filled a phonebook sized guide that lay in the trunk of every cruiser, seldom to never hauled out for a reference, like a high school grammar textbook on the shelf.

Mick had been absolutely brazened with the high five move. Was he looking to be fired? It made Joe wonder how *the blue wall of silence* here compared with what he'd known in the Midwest.

Investigator Perkins came into the bedroom with several Ziploc bags of prescription pills that she set on the bed next to her clipboard. "Lawler, check my count and countersign before I seal the meds up."

"Sure thing, *Sergeant* Perkins."

Perkins shot him a look. Then sighed. "I'm sorry. It's just that my brain is multi-tasking and I've gone into checklist mode. Let me try again. Officer Lawler, would you please check my count and countersign before I seal the meds up."

"It'll be my pleasure," Joe said. He knew that it was legal SOP for a police officer to assist and witness the Coroner's Investigation on scene until completed. Then the police would take over for as far as it went. But he wasn't going to allow himself to be disrespected by a peer. Perkins turned her attention back to the decedent. Performing a textbook full hands-on physical examination of the body as Lawler had been taught in class. She took pictures from various angles and distances, and finally she wrote down notes.

The other agency officers chatted or made small shop talk for a little while, then were called or drifted away back to their jurisdictions. Some shook hands and said g'bye. Some didn't.

"It is looking like a straight suicide," Perkins said. "He didn't leave a note. But I spoke on his phone to his ex, and some work friends. They all said he'd expressed suicidal ideations since he was separated and laid off from his job. And he's been drinking heavily, mixing it with prescription drugs. We all know that in theory you treat every death scene as a homicide until proven otherwise. But I'm pretty sure we've got a suicide here. You may want to bounce it off your detectives or call out your evidence folks. Up to you, but I'm almost done here."

Against Mick's advice, Joe dialed the on-call Stewart investigator, Detective Barry Duk. *Rhymes with a winter hat toque*, Joe recalled what Mick had said of the man. *And Duk hated that some called him Detective Duck behind his back.* It didn't help that he wore oversized white or tan three-piece suits and was a fat fuck who waddled when he walked. But he was a favorite of the Chief, and that he cherished his mostly nine-to-five, plain clothes gig.

Lawler tried to fill Duk in on the scene.

"Jeez kid, what time is it?"

Lawler bristled. He was older and had more police and investigative experience than this guy.

"Look, Joe is it? Look, you go to the autopsy in the morning," Duk ordered him. "Call me then, *if* they find anything suspicious. Otherwise fuck the fuck off!"

The call ended. Joe pictured Duk at the other end of the call, punching the disconnect hard and slamming the phone down.

"Told'ja, Joe." Mick said without any bile or irony.

Joe turned back to the corpse at hand, saying to Mick, "Guess Detective Duck's not big on dead with eyes, drooling mouths, swollen tongues, and red stretched, bent necks, or fresh, raw ligature marks, eh, Mick?"

"Nor too fond of broken nails from clawing at a rope or cord?

Perkins came back into the bedroom carrying a kitchen step stool. "Would you two Stuart's Finest please hold him up and then ease him down when I cut the ligature?" She'd brought her black doctor's bag back with her. Mick and Joe moved to help her.

She took out her Leatherman pliers and wire cutter and climbed onto the steps getting ready to cut the cord all the way at the top, where it was looped over and behind the door. Then she thought better of it, folded the cutters, and slid out the awl blade. Using the awl, she pried and undid the knotted cord from the door hinge. Campanella fell, if not like a ton of bricks, then like the dead weight he was.

They almost dropped him but then managed to lay him on the floor on his back. To their surprise Perkins started another full body exam. Top to bottom, and front to back. Joe thought, *This lady's damn thorough.*

Then, as if on cue, two funeral home drivers with "Murphy's Funeral Home" embroidered on their matching pale blue polo shirts appeared with a metal gurney on wheels. They produced a heavy black body bag, laid it out next to Mr. Campanella, and lined it with a clean white sheet. Then they collapsed the gurney until the bed was inches from the floor. Under Perkins' watchful gaze, they carefully placed him inside, zipped him up, placed him on the gurney, and raised it up again.

Once everyone was outside the house, Perkins asked, "You fellas done here?"

"Yep, since Duk's not coming," Mick said in a tone of both assurance and resolve.

"I guess so." Lawler agreed, knowing that once a door was closed on a death investigation that it was seldom opened again.

Perkins locked the door behind them. Then approached the van drivers, who had opened the back doors, and were running the gurney at the open back, like they were young wizards pushing their school gear full steam at a brick wall marked: *Platform 9-3/4.*

The front gurney support legs hit the bumper and van tailgate, folding, collapsing the wheels under the gurney bed. The back legs and the wheel hit, bam, undoing the locks. In fact, the mechanism locked the gurney down to the van floor, secured the doors. The men turned to face Perkins.

"Thanks guys. Take him back to our office and leave him in the intake garage. I have to run across town to notify his sister, NOK." She turned to Mick and Lawler. "Some things are best done in person. Not over a phone."

Goodbyes were said. Hands shaken. And they watched the navy-blue, unmarked Murphy's van and the white officially marked CCCO SUV drive off in each's sure direction.

"*Whataya* say we go for coffee?" Joe suggested.

Mick stared at Joe who stared back and asked, "What?"

"Come on Officer Joe. Let's get back to the barn and get this report done, so we can go home without being yelled at for too much overtime. Tomorrow is my day off."

"Mine too," said Lawler, shrugging.

FIVE

10-2: good radio signal

Lawler wound his throttle forward and back as he descended the winding mountain roads from what he'd learned locals called the 'Red Planet landscape' of what Lawler'd been told was the *Valley of Fire*, which took him northeast of metropolitan Las Vegas. His orange and black Harley Davidson *Livewire* electric motorcycle sounded deafening in the surrounding silence of the desert, its high-pitched whoosh-to-whine rivaling the Air Force fighter jets that so frequently maneuvered between Nellis Air Force Base and a place the local referred to as Area Fifty-One, an elaborate entertainment area *where anything goes* or went.

Joe'd been between cell tower service, but as he approached the outskirts of the city, he heard several soft buzzing notifications in his helmet, his Bluetooth, which he'd named *Harold*. His iPhone was clipped to his handlebars, so he could see several missed calls and texts from the Stewart Nevada Police Department, where he'd maintained employment in his part-time capacity as a police officer on the weekend *power shift*, 4pm to 2am, for the past six months, not too long after he had retired from his mid-west job at the Morainal Hills Police Department, on the Wisconsin-Illinois border. A damned cold environment.

Here and now, Lawler enjoyed a balmy 63-degree November day in Southern Nevada, and he did not miss shoveling snow and scraping his car windshield in winter back *home*.

Another call came through and he told Harold Bluetooth to "accept."

"Where have you been, Lawler? The Chief wants to see you." Daisy Reed, also known as Daisy Dukes behind her back, was the Admin to Chief Lewis, and had been with Stewart PD for some seven years, since she had retired as a Nevada State Police Trooper, up in Eiko County. She pretty much ran all of the SPD day-to-day and admin. And if the next city elections went well for her, she could end up as the new Chief.

"Now? It's my day off." Lawler tried to speak loudly over the wind and bike noise that swept into his helmet.

"Ten minutes ago."

"I'm on my bike coming back from VOF." He said, using the abbreviation for Valley of Fire. "I'm still about 40 minutes out."

"Well you'd better get in here as fast as you can. Chief is not a happy camper."

"Good copy. Any idea why?"

"Something to do with the email you sent him about your other job applications."

"Roger that." Lawler used the slang, rather than official local code "copy" in an attempt at bravado and to make light of the Chief's summons. But perhaps he should have heeded conventional wisdom and not said anything about his other job applications until it was time to request a hopefully positive recommendation.

"I'm headed straight in. I'll be there as fast as I can." He caught himself almost saying "Lawler out." But didn't.

He could see the Las Vegas strip in the near distance, from Downtown and the Stratosphere at the North End, to the Harry Reid, formerly McCarron, Airport across from the Luxor at Mandalay Bay near the South end.

In the middle, he could see the rainbow lit High Roller Ferris wheel gondolas, and MSG Sphere, which now had a highly animated and brightly colored giant snow globe image on its high- definition dome surface. And something new, He could see jolly red mini skirted Santa dancers in high heeled boots, the Vegas version of the Radio City Rockettes dancing in an ever-circling hologram above the Millenium Casino, where the Riviera used to be so bright. One constant in Vegas was *change*.

Normally, he liked to cruise down the strip on his way through Paradise Nevada north of the Sahara Casino, and his small, single bedroom condo in Stewart City, but this time he was focused on speeding as quickly as possible down the Interstate 15 and I-515, back to Stewart Police Station before Chief Lewis grew antsier and madder. The Harley *Livewire* had a top speed of 110. But Lawler just pushed it as fast as he could at the allowed speed, weaving in and out of traffic, trying not to attract the attention of either State Troopers or Vegas Metro patrolling the highway.

Maybe his Stewart part time badge, or retired Morainal Hills badge might cut him some kind of professional courtesy or a break. But maybe not. Either way, he didn't want to be stopped, to then be even later in responding to the Chief.

Of course, traffic was jammed up by the spaghetti bowl curves and exits. There was a pending law to rescind the law allowing motorcycles to lane split between cars, but it had not passed yet. Lawler lane split at will, rating dirty looks from the cars and trucks slowed by traffic, jealous, he imagined of his getting past with such ease.

He used his gate opener for the private lot behind the station and used his thumbprint to open the biometric lock on the back door. He took off his helmet and started combing his hair in the glass frame reflection of the Stewart Municipal Street map on the hallway corkboard outside the Chief's door. Daisy was smartly dressed in a dress shirt and brown blazer. She had a fresh haircut like the singer Pink. Long pompadour in front, and severe on the sides and back. "Lawler's here." She said into the intercom on the phone.

Lawler shot her a look, because he wasn't done with his hair, and wanted to first make a pit stop to the restroom. Too late now.

"You'd better go in," Daisy said.
Lawler took off his gray nylon and Kevlar coat and set it along with his Shark adjustable bike helmet, which he placed on the chair in front of Daisy's desk.

"Lawler!" came the high-pitched Lewis voice from inside his office, but Joe was already walking toward the open door.

Officer Mick Finnegan, aka "Mick the Trick" walked by with a cup of coffee. "I warned you." he said without slowing. *"Tsk...tsk."*

Gabe Lewis looked up, not even pretending to be busy with work papers or making Lawler wait. Stewart PD wasn't a particularly formal department and didn't stand on military discipline or any pretense of protocol, but Lawler thought he would remain standing this time, out of respect, until Lewis icily said, "Sit down, Joe." Lawler sat in one of the lightly padded modern metal chairs in front of Lewis' desk.

"What is this email you sent me about applying for other jobs? Metro, Henderson, North Las Vegas, Clark County Coroner's Investigator, City Marshall. And Constable? Constable! Constable is an elected position. Are you a politician now?"

"Politician? I'd rather be dead," replied Joe.

Guess you're too green around here to know Clark County Constables are elected for four years," began the chief. "They work on a fee-plus-mileage basis at no expense to the taxpayer. Constables serve the courts. Small claims, summons, evictions, bank account-wage garnishments, and other crap in which a suit is started in civil cases."

"Well, I was just looking to increase my income. Vegas is *ahh*, has a high rate of—"

"You're not happy working here with us? You want to move on?"

"I like working here. And I'm grateful for the opportunity. But this is a part-time badge with no medical or other benefits. I need something full-time. I'm not planning on leaving. I would keep the part-time position here, if allowed."

"Then why this email?"

"I just wanted to be aboveboard, give you a heads up. In case, you know, if verification of current employment and recommendation letters start coming in."

"That sounds pretty optimistic of you. You're assuming a lot." Lewis looked down at his laptop, as if rereading the email. "And I'm not thrilled with your job performance here lately."

"I've only been here six months." *And I've got twenty-five years of experience. More than you,* Lawler thought but bit his tongue.

"My performance, Sir?" Lawler asked.

"You're assigned the power shift on weekend nights. Your job is visible patrol, calls as assigned, and write preventative traffic and community order citations."

"Yes sir." Lawler waited as Lewis stared at him. "I got

all top marks on my first department evaluation last month."

"Yes, yes. But what else have you been doing?"

Hell, I don't drink any more than the other officers, Joe thought. *Haven't been involved in any domestic incidents. My interaction with the public always positive, except when it wasn't. And maybe I took a little longer on lunch and coffee breaks than the regs outline, but no more than the other departmental officers here at Stewart PD.*

You've been out playing detective. Knocking on doors, bothering the public. Trying to show off and turn mountains into molehills."

"Don't you mean molehills into mountains, Sir?"

"Whatever! You're supposed to be out on proactive and visible patrol and assignments, in uniform. You are not Metro homicide or CSI. That damned phony Crime Scene Investigation nonsense all over TV shows now! Hell, there's no such designation in the real world for—*whata* they call it? Crime Scene Analyst Investigator?"

"I'm just trying to do a thorough job. Sir," Lawler defended.

"Thorough, *eh*? You're treating Peter DePalma like a killer while his wife is alive!"

"She's still in a coma, but what's put her there remains a mystery."

"Damnit, Joe, that's what I'm talking about. You're not called on to be the Sherlock Holmes of Stewart PD. Only if Betty DePalma dies, only then can it even be theorized as possible homicide."

"Meanwhile, DePalma knows from true crime TV that the first 24 to 48 hours are critical, so he took his sweet time calling 911. Why? And as for me, my actions, I was assigned to take the supposed car-burglary reports at Shasta Condominiums. Knocking on doors and finding potential witnesses is just SOP, right?"

"Are you saying our investigators doing standard operations? Aren't doing their jobs?"

"Nothing like that, Sir." Actually, Joe was thinking precisely that. "It's just that they are awfully busy, and there is never enough manpower hours, so I try to pitch in to be helpful whenever I can. I've always believed in proactive policing and following every lead, before coming to conclusions."

"Do the job you are being paid to do, and maybe, just maybe, you'll be in line when we have a full-time position opening up here. Understand?"

"Yes, Sir."

"Get out of my office."

"Yessir. Thank you."

Lawler shut the Chief's door behind him. Daisy was away from her desk. Mick the Trick was playing with

Joe's helmet. Toggling up the full facial visor, flicking the Maverick pilot style polarized sun lens portion up and down into the recesses of the helmet, and back again behind the clear wind lens.

"Fancy," Mick said. "Can I take your bike for a ride some time? I've never ridden an electric Harley ever before."

"Uh-huh," Lawler non-committedly said.

Lawler wanted to take his helmet from Mick, get on his bike and go home. But he had to first hit the head. Mick followed him in.

"I warned you not to do up any fancy reports on all those follow-ups you were doing to the burglary and domestic—"

"Potential homicide."

"Potential homicide." Mick agreed. "But you're still on probation. They can fire you for any reason, or for no reason. Without legal cause or departmental cause."

Lawler, finished, washed his hands at the not dirty, but not pristine sink.

SIX

Out for Post: Shift break at Stewart NV, Post 7, Evel Pie.

Lawler knew that the autoerotic deaths of men, old and young, single or partnered, in Vegas, or Anytown USA, was not at all unusual, but he learned that was especially true in high stat-wise Vegas. *Blue Vegas*—they even had a name for it here. At a coffee break, Mick told Joe all about it. "Don't matter if he's a high roller, good or bad luck, a CEO or the poor janitorial staff fellow, or failed actor to underpaid social worker, the 'alone' man without family or a steady group of acquaintances, be it old buddies or co-workers, brought him to this sad end of life in Neon City."

Joe thought Mick was conflating suicides with accidental autoerotic deaths by misadventure, but nodded and said, "Kinda like young runaways on the West Coast who gravitate to Hollywood, and young runaways on the East Coast who gravitate to Daytona Beach and even Hollywood, Florida, thinking it a movie town when that's as far from the truth as it gets."

Mick lightly laughed and sipped at his coffee. "*Many's a* runaway gravitates *back* to where their best memories come to mind: warm temps, bright lights, properly made drinks, noisy gambling tables, and the young prostitute met at a Las Vegas bar."

After ordering a second coffee and a slice of apple pie, Mick added, "Hell, sure teens run to beaches, sure, but the average age of autoerotic victims is in the early thirties. Elderly victims of more than sixty-five are not terribly uncommon in Vegas. Guys with…*whataya-ma* call it, oh yeah, suicidal ideation. They often return to Vegas. You know, to party and then take pills or shoot themselves."

"Make some kind of twisted sense, I guess," replied Lawler.

"Oddly enough, most Vegas autoerotic deaths are relatively young to middle aged locals in their own homes, engaged in solo sex play. And there're some strangulation and breath play at Vegas and California *fetish'n'bondage* sex clubs. Never took a death call at one, not as far as I remember…."

"Think you'd remember a call like that, Mick."

"Accidental? Misadventure? With help, so maybe involuntary manslaughter? Indifference to life. Could turn into a real *cann'a'* piss and shit."

The more Mick talked, the more he gave himself away as a burnout in this job, and perhaps in this town. Perhaps having Joe to train was good for Mick, who had now to educate his 'trainee', which he enjoyed calling Lawler, despite Joe's being older than him. But the experienced Chicago area cop took it well, knowing that every town, city, and province in the country had its own parameters and idiosyncrasies, so a bit of ribbing and tutelage was in fact appreciated and understood.

While every precinct in Chicago alone was different in many ways, there remained a certain sure-cop attitude that cops shared across the nation: a defining set of characteristics, somewhat like the defining set carried by military men and women, certain bedrock character qualities, some of which were good, and some not so good. Either way, the character *set* was there for a person to live by.

These were bedrock traits that made Lawler and guys like Mick, stuck in a kind of self-induced entrancement, so certain of their own sure streetwiseness that they could not entertain a new or fresh or different view of a set of facts presented to them, especially when the same symptoms of the blue nodding heads got together to drink to their collective intra-genotype thinking. This amounted to a closed, cold, and hard mind-set in the face of death, giving it the finger, even railing at it. At the same time, the same cop could cuddle a stray dog, or some poor kid who'd just witnessed his mother murdered by his father or stepdad, or the 'boyfriend'.

Mick's hand-held radio crackled to life and Daisy's voice came on, announcing a nearby residence with an unusual odor emanating from it—according to an Amazon delivery boy who'd dropped off a package. She gave Mick the address and went silent. Mick was not leaving until he finished his pie.

Lawler smelled the insistent odor that'd assailed the Amazon delivery kid even through the door. It clawed at his nostrils and recalled to mind Dr. Coran's decomp class here in the field. An awful aroma, the odor seemingly rising from the Pullman kitchen. No, it was in the small dining nook. He smelled it so much sooner than he could identify the *jellifying* pot roast on the table alongside flies laying eggs in the leftover mash potatoes and green beans. The last supper it appeared. To let the others know he had brass, Lawler pointed to the desiccated meat and said, "*Rump Roast*, be my guest. Dig in, boys!"

But the joke immediately choked within his chest and in his heart as a bad and an unnecessary remark. *I coulda let that thought pass without saying it out loud,* he told himself now. *Coulda left that one for Mick the Trick.* At the same time, it won laughter from all those in the place except the dead. Even so, the dark joke made Lawler one of the guys.

A collective sigh of relief came over the men amid this rotting, decomp smell, and Lawler, along with the others felt they'd been fooled by the odor emanating from the rotted meat, thinking the foul odor could get no worse until they arrived at the bedroom. It was here that the stench could get no worse. They'd been wrong about the roast.

The dead men before them now had the feel of stray dogs. They appeared sadly two older guys having a last *hoo-rah* in Tinsel Town. "Just two old kike boyfriends," Mick dully called out the scene, adding, "Kinda funny both going together like this. Hard to believe."
Lawler nodded, handkerchief over his nose. "How do you know they're Jewish, Mick?"

"Passport. One flew in from *Is-ray-el*."

"Don't believe there has ever been a double autoerotic death…"

"If it is a double this time, it will be unique and notable. Interesting story for the guys back at the station."

A sergeant that Lawler had not met had come on scene just behind them, introduced as Sergeant Stobile, who, on having eavesdropped on them, casually said, regarding the two dead men, "Love knows no bounds, right, Mick?"

"Not even the next dimension, you mean?"

"Right, *mah* man!"

One thing cops everywhere held in common, Lawler thought–*dark humor gone bad.*

SEVEN

10-4: Copy that/All's quiet (on the Western front) Stewart NV.

The next night shift patrol had them at what Mick called, "The lull before the storm." And sure enough Daisy dispatched them to an address they were nearest to, pulling from Mick, "Aha! Yet another run-of-the-mill *old fart* suicide call."

It was far more in the category of dull for Mick after so many more years here in Vegas than Lawler. That was for certain. "Every damn night. Same *old man* shit. But last night man! That was weird...two guys, two harnesses, couldn't even take turns. Might've spotted *one'nutther* if they, you know, had taken turns...*ahh* hell."

Mick fell silent after his brief rant. And after all his squabbling about the *same-o-same-o* calls. But once inside this apartment, there felt a different atmosphere and feel to the case. The victim was a young black man, seemingly in his twenties, and it seemed a staged suicide by gunshot to the brain via the mouth. Staged it seemed, as the gun had magically remained clamped in his hand, the barrel still in his mouth. The magical part: *no recoil*.

Investigating further into the darker areas of hallway and bedrooms and bath, Lawler uncovered in one bedroom what looked like a jam-filled Costco warehouse of as yet *still-in-the-box* goods and equipment.

Lawler called for Mick to come have a look-see. Mick, weapon drawn, did so, and on seeing the huge stash of goods, he whistled and took a deep breath. "Shit," began Mick, "we'll never figure out where all this came from."

The body on the blow-up mattress in the front room had a halo of brain matter and so much blood that the dead man had become one with the mattress. But that problem could be left to the coroner's boys and girls, certainly Mick felt so, as he began going from box to box, saying, "Take what you want, Joe, before any prudes show up! Look here, a case of JB Scotch, damn, my favorite. Taking it to the car. Give me the keys for the trunk."

For a silent moment, Joe just stared in disbelief at Mick.

"Really? Stealing from the dead? From a crime scene? We've talked about this. In this day and age of cameras everywhere, defund the police, brass and state attorneys willing to end your career and throw you under the bus without a moment's hesitation, and witnesses everywhere, fuck, man! Cell phone cameras and gosh knows what else can trip you up, you are *not* going to pull this shit on my watch. I don't know if you are so burned out you are trying to deliberately end your career. But you are not taking me with you."

"Hey, easy, Joe. I only—"

"Mick this ain't the bad old days. Sure, some of the troops will look the other way for gray areas, like use of force, or pimply department regs. But there is nothing worse than a thief with a badge, and no one's going to look the other way for that."

"Point made, Joe…"

"Atop that, if you have no ethics or pride in the privilege of being able to do a job that many want and few can get, and most couldn't do if they did, then do us all a favor and just quit and pull the pin now!"

Mick scowled going from surprise, to anger, to perplexed. He opened his mouth to say something then shut it. Then he stormed off—calling over his shoulder: "I'm going out for a cigarette. Back when I'm back."

When Mick had returned, he muttered, "Ahh, shit, Joe, you're right." He then lifted the crate of liquor and hefted it to back to where he'd found it. When he came back, still no one else had arrived at the scene. Meanwhile Lawler felt sure that the neighborhood Robin Hood, dead in the front room, was no suicide. The caller who'd tipped the police off to the scene had remained an anonymous Amazon delivery man.

Joe and Mick had been dispatched to a *check-well-being* call at the Sea Breeze apartments on East Shady Lane. It had always struck Mick as he'd said on the way here that "It's an odd location for a small two-story light brown brick apartment building of six units."

"How so?"

"The apartments are in a commercial district, behind a strip mall anchored by a Walgreens, next to an Office

Depot, Dollar Store, and currently, an empty, out-of-season *Spirit Halloween* shop. There's a ten-foot chain link fence topped by barbed wire barely separating apartment residents from the back of the strip mall."

Lawler stared out the window down on a series of loading docks, forklifts, dumpsters, old wood pallets and various detritus. There were some green and white plastic privacy strips still left woven into the chain link from when the fence was first installed. Broken spots gave the fence a gap-tooth look.

"Think I know where the TVs and JB boxes came from, Mick, and our line of *suspects*, may be."

When Mick came closer, Lawler pointed to the row of back doors and loading docks below. "Musta been one hell of a temptation."

"You really do think you're here to play *Columbo*, don't you, Lawler. You know how damn much paperwork is involved in a homicide? Opposed to a suicide, I mean."

They did their part as the CCCO Investigator came and went with the funeral van crew taking the body. With nary a further word between them about the box goods.

EIGHT

Code: 410-2 safety status check/you okay?

A week later

Every night in the MHPD area Joe Lawler had vehicular emergencies and calls to get ambulances running *to and fro*, usually to the closest hospital for taking in horribly maimed and traumatized individuals, often dead-on-arrival. In the greater Vegas area, it was not so much about death by vehicle as it was by small-time, petty operatives and by suicide. Here, Joe saw many more suicides or death by autoerotic *play* that'd gone terribly wrong than he ever had in Illinois.

Lawler pulled into the uncurbed gravel roadside that adjoined a dozen or so gravel parking spaces for residents and guests. The check well-being request had been made by an anonymous neighbor who reported that Mr. Frank Gunderson, 320 Shady Lane, Apartment 2C, had not been seen leaving for several days. There were six mailboxes next to the locked front entry door, and the one marked "Gunders. 2C" was overflowing with envelopes, mailers, junk mail out onto the front step, where almost a week's worth of newspapers lay, some open and blowing in the wind. The man's ripped, black, vinyl-topped Impala with the sun worn avocado green paint job was parked in front.

Lawler randomly pressed apartment call buttons several times, answering the "Yeah?" or "Who is it?" and "What?" with "Police." and "Police business." each time. Third try was the charm, the door finally buzzing. He pushed the foyer door open and entered the building. He trod the thick stained carpet up one flight of stairs and knocked on the door to apartment 2C. No answer. He listened inside, and he heard the feint sound, likely a television show. He knocked louder only to arouse a dog from sleep to angry, wild barking. He looked in though a partially fogged peep hole, realizing himself the fool, as no one could see though from the outside, but at his toes, at the door bottom slit, he saw a flickering light. Probably a television.

When Sergeant Ben Stobile arrived with Mick in tow, Lawler was making several failed attempts to kick in the apartment's front door. "You were damn quick," Lawler said.

"I had already started drifting this way before Central dispatched me." Stobile was sizing up the front door, which had not just one, but two deadbolt security locks in addition to the locking doorknob. As Mick was no match for the door, Stobile said, "Stand back, boys. Allow me." He kicked the door a few times, and the three of them noticed that no part of the door even so much as flexed on the lock to doorjamb side. So, Stobile stepped back as far as the narrow hallway allowed and threw his weight and his shoulder into the other side of the door, and the big man knocked the back side off its hinges, all in a shower of wood shards and splinters.

"That's how you do it!" Stobile crowed, refusing to admit to any pain, or rub his hurt shoulder.

"Hope you didn't injure yourself, John," said a grinning Mick. "You're no fullback no more."

"I'm just fine." Nevertheless, he stood rubbing the shoulder.

Stobile and Lawler both noticed four facts. One, the door had a locking latch inside at top and bottom, in addition to the deadbolts. Two, the television in the living room was up rather loud, on a Tela-sale/infomercial type channel. Three, the godawful stench of rotting putrefying meat. And four, the dog was locked in a room somewhere else.

"I think you've got *one!*" Sergeant Stobile told Lawler, meaning Joe'd be in charge and responsible for all aspects, including the paperwork. Or was he jokingly referring to this scene having only one suicide *vic* this time around.

There was an eat-in kitchen adjacent to the living area. On the small Formica table, there was an array of items: glass, plate, utensils, salt and pepper shakers, and a dog-eared thriller entitled *Primal Instinct*. The plate was strewn with unfinished vegetables and an entree of turkey from what appeared a frozen dinner turned out on the plate. Green beans, and mashed potatoes. A serving plate for one at a folding table.

"Who doesn't like a good bird for dinner, eh?" Stobile beat Lawler to the obvious joke. Then they searched the rest of the apartment, and they found two bedrooms in the back. One kept the dog from being shot, as he or she was being loud and scrapping at the door. Mick joked,

"If I owned half that dog, I'd shoot my half."

One bedroom was completely filled with boxed and blister packed, brand new unopened store merchandise. There were no furnishings of any kind, but every wall was stacked, some double deep to the ceiling with boxes and store goods.

"What the hell?" mused Joe. "This looks too damn familiar, Mick."

There were no price tags, receipts, or anything indicating where the boxes may have come from. There were car mufflers, hubcaps, radios, seat covers, pot and pan sets, spice racks, flowerpots, bathtub rubber shower matts, scrub brushes, bulk boxes of dish soap and cleanser and a variety of other store goods.

"What the fuck?" Joe asked again. "Is there a black-market sale going on I don't know about? This is the second place we've entered in like eight days filled with goodies, right Mick?"

"Organized gang robberies. The big guy in charge, the entrepreneur pays a guy to stow the stash," Mick explained the coincidence.

"Yeah, get a clue, Lawman," Stobile bluntly added.

"This goes on to this degree here?" Joe asked.

"You sayin' it don't happen in *Chicagoland*?"

"Not saying it doesn't happen in and around Chicago, no, but we were on top of it there."

Stobile defensively shot back: "Newshounds got it wrong then, I guess."

This guy's a real ass, Lawler thought but kept it to himself.

They then checked a third bedroom. There was a decomposing man lying in the bed, face up, and covered from foot to shoulders in clean, newly minted sheets, blankets, and quilt. It was hotter back here than the rest of the apartment, and the stench became increasingly overwhelming. Double overwhelming–. Lawler went over to the bedroom window, threw the curtains back, and he next tried to open the window to let in some air. But the wood window and casement were painted over several times, and effectively painted and glued shut, along with four carefully spaced nails. "No paranoia here," he muttered.

The decomposing and rotted meat smell of the dead human being under the covers was unbearable to Lawler. Stobile stepped between Lawler and the window, and with the meaty side of his hand wrapped in a towel, he slammed his fist through the glass, the air pouring in as if on a mission. The window moorings, paint and nails meant nothing now. *Gone with the Wind* came to mind; if only the stench was that easy to kill. Not even the fresh air could end it. The decomp smell wasn't going away, but it was a bit better. Less heat eased the odor.

Mick, clearly having trouble with the stench, stepped outside where he picked up the mail to be of some help for later investigative purposes. While outside, Mick knocked on a few neighbor doors to get any information he might, asking about comings, goings, maybe next of kin, but he returned with little to no information, except that, "He was an okay fella, minded his own business, and waved from time to time."

They all knew their places in the hierarchy of the department, that the coroner would ultimately notify next of kin in this case. No info about bedroom warehouse would be released to anyone, and especially not the press; nothing of store goods, for sure, as their rightful owners might never be determined. The deceased had in a journal declared himself 'retired for all *intent and purpose*, been retired for a while, and no one from *work give one shit bout me,* a hamburger-hotdog joint called *Mustard's Last Stand. Hate* the boss *and so the place*, should *light it up*, although he added in the dog-eared journal that the cook was a master of the bistro cuisine, adding a *great thanks to Jose, the Mexican cook there.*

Lawler who'd begun reading snippets of the journal, looking for whatever he could determine useful, realized there was nothing about how or why the decedent had a warehouse of goods in his home. Or why he'd committed suicide. The assumption was he'd set up his own small business, selling stolen goods from home in his self-imposed *retirement*.

When the coroner's investigator arrived, she introduced herself as Kathy Quales Loudin, and she wore a tailored suit, dress shirt, and a string tie with a turquoise broach, picture I.D. clipped to her suit jacket. Easily recognizing Joe, she near curtsied, said hello with a surprised look that quickly faded when she immediately got to work.

She pulled back the sheet, blankets and quilt, and the bloated puffy dead man looked as though he might pop. He was naked except for a pair of striped pajama pants, watch and three gold rings. The bloated flesh made removal of the watch and rings, which were made for wrist and fingers a lot smaller than his fingers and wrist were now. Loudin took a photo of the watch and rings and said into her iPhone reorder, "Impossible to perform on scene. There's heavy angry maroon-red, rigor mortis creeping upward all around the deceased man's ears, lower neck and jaw, shoulders, arms, suspect back as well, other unmentionable areas where the blood's been pulled down by gravity, pooling at the bottom of the male body where he lays on the bed."

The funeral home driver from Murphy's was new. A very short thin man, he looked about to drop of malnourishment. Joe thought it not unlikely he was on the wrong side of a growing meth problem.

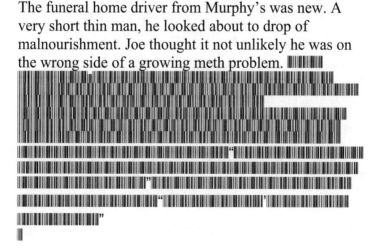

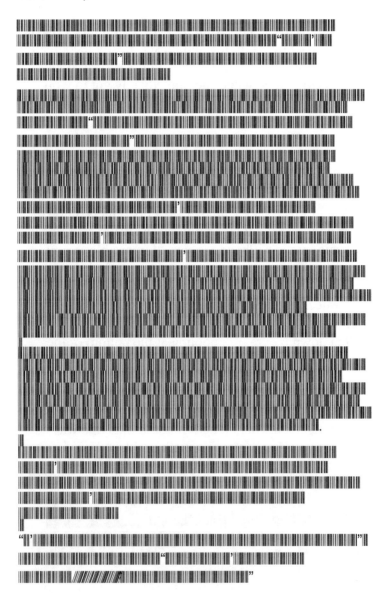

"Meaning exactly?" asked Mick.

"Meaning that his body has dripped into the mattress ticking and material, then dried into the bedding. Again!" Lawler added, gritting his teeth.

Stobile, his face pinched, urged for Mick to help. "Let's all give it another tug."

This time, they jerked and twisted, pulled and tugged, even as the awful noise of the body and mattress separating sounded an alarming *to-the-ear* cross between dismembering a thanksgiving turkey and slowly cracking thick stalks of celery. There was even the sound of ripping Velcro being separated. Having been on crime and horror film sets as an extra, Lawler recalled how the sound effect guys would so often join one sound with another, sampling noises: *irks* and *who*hahhs, putting them in a digital mixer to make the extended and repeated squishing, ripping, and then the winning sound, *shqwuercchh*. It felt, or rather sounded the same to Joe, and surely the others gathered here felt the sound running down their spines by now.

Lawler thought the smell was bad, but this *pop group* of the dead proved unreal. And it increased bit-by-bit, as they ripped, tore, and wobbled the body separate from the mattress, releasing all the more body smells into the air. And the physical manifestation of this massive stench wasn't just routine bloat and decomposition. Where the blood encrusted livor mortis had burst, when the dry coagulated scab joining the back of the body to the mattress was ripped apart like two halves of this human Velcro. Once separated, there was left on the man's back, and on the mattress and sheets, a grayish red goop, the color of melted brains. Like bloody gray, red-roasted meat drippings left at the bottom of a baking pan.

They pulled and slid the body into the bag, along with the soaked bottom fitted sheet. Mick saw to the stretched corners, somewhat distancing himself, and Joe couldn't blame him. The coroner's assistant toe tagged him, and much to the relief of all present when he was zipped up, it helped with the odor a little. The skinny van driver steered the gurney down the stairs, *bump-bump da bump* loudly, with the Coroner and Cops guiding and providing some drag so this didn't turn into an old Mack Sennett comedy scene. Luckily, despite the noise, no citizens stuck a head from apartment windows or doors, nor did any brave soul step out to see them dragging and thumping the body on the gurney down the stairs.

NINE

Code 11-11: returning to station w/VIP,
Cochise.

The old man's suicide note, in difficult to read cursive, left an impact even on Mick as it read:

Officers, I'm sorry to be trouble. My girlfriend left
cause I can't stop drinking and other stuff I'm not gonna
say. Please be good to Cochise. Don't take him to no
fking pound, please. He's a good boy, and he'll be
scared and confused. Dog food is on the counter. I will
feed him before I go, but he will be hungry again by time
you find me.

The dog, Cochise, proved as wonderful a people-person animal as the dead man had promised. He was a terrier mix with God knew what, and as soon as they'd opened the door, he'd raced to be with his master even in death. It had taken a good deal of coaxing to get him to come along, coaxing and dog treats. Mick had taken a true liking to the little fellow, the two bonding. Mick had also told Daisy that they were coming into the station with a perp, finishing with Cochise, which Daisy literally clapped at in response, as she had been pushing Chief Lewis for a full set of new codes to replace the old ones, code names of famous indigenous American Indians such as Geronimo, Cochise, Quanah Parker, Red Cloud and other greats like Sitting Bull and Crazy Horse. Only the Coroner can arrest or initially remove a Sheriff from office.

"You know you shouldn't get her hopes up like that, Mick."

"I know but can't help myself."

"Maybe she'll take the dog. Might be good for what's going on with her."

Maybe…if I don't claim him first." Hearing this, Cochise leapt from backseat to Mick's lap."

"You think Daisy's not long for Stewart PD. Given it's run by Lewis, I mean."

"*Dunno*, but she told me that her inner child has always been male, so who's to judge?" He scratched under the dog's chin, and Cochise loved it. Watching Mick with the dog and the dog with Mick, Lawler doubted that the two would ever be separated, not even by Daisy.

As it turned out, Chief Lewis had been in earshot of Daisy and the banter about Cochise, and as a result he blew his stack, thinking that Daisy had initiated her idea regarding official calls using American Indigenous hero names from Sacagawea to Cochise, after his having officiously shot the idea down.

Her idea had come after she had seen the film *Killers of the Flower Moon*. By the time Joe and Mick had arrived, Lewis had Daisy in tears.

Joe and Mick, on learning this, went directly into Lewis' office to introduce him to Cochise, where the pooch had come from, and that Cochise had adopted Mick. Lewis, in a rare moment of remorse, went for the ladies' room in search of Daisy to actually apologize.

***

The more that Mick and Joe got to work together, the more they swapped cop tales, the more they began to like and respect one another. Lawler told tales of various incidents and politics seeping into stationhouses in Illinois, in towns small and large, in the burbs and in Chicago. "Legislatures *wanna* control the precincts same as they want to control our schools there."

They were on lunch break at a place called *The Red Lion*, British cuisine, specialty mincemeat pie. "Not much different here," Mick assured Lawler over his shepherd's pie.

"Mick, you got nothing on what we had to deal with where I come from."

"Okay, go ahead, shoot!"

"Kid you not, the sheriff and the coroner in Lake County, Illinois had term limits, right?"

"That's a good thing, Joe, term limits."

"Normally, sure, but these two politicians would take turns running for either office every other term."

"As bad as that sounds buddy, currently, in all of Nye County, Nevada, adjacent to Las Vegas, and in some parts of Clark County here, a judge or magistrate is not required by law to have a college, *or* law degree."

"*G'damn!*" Lawler said, having picked it up from Coran.

"Talk of mandating an educational requirement getting nowhere. Always fails, because it's impossible to find qualified candidates for out of the way county jurisdictions in desert areas."

The discussion shifted to their sheer number of suicide cases in and around Vegas, which Mick called a final symptom of the *Vegas Blues* to which Lawler commented on the ones who foolishly put bags over their heads thinking that they could contain some mess from headshot wounds."

"Yeah, and how they dress in their best and use makeup or lay out their best clothes for the funeral."

"And how they put the driver's license on their chest or in their pockets to assist us with I.D. and Mick, none of that's been happening lately, like with the double auto erotica fellas."

"First, they had no pockets on '*em,* and second, they didn't expect to be going that far is why no laying out of their funeral clothes."

"Who's playing detective now?"

"That scene still botherin' you, ain't it, Joe?"

"Like a recurrent nightmare, yeah. Something about it, yeah."

"Like what? What?" Mick downed his coffee.

"Two guys, knowing how dangerous that tripping is…they'd have taken turns *spotting* one another, Mick. And I checked over the photos. How could either of them tie their hands together the way they were found? And wallets empty of cash and cards? *Betcha* someone used those cards long after… and what if they were supposed to be *spotted* by a third party who left them like that? Depraved indifference to life, the prosecutors in Illinois and New York call it."

Mick held up a hand to Joe, asking for silence, as his hand-held crackled to life. Daisy reporting on a death scene on a corner street they were near, adding,

"Chicano garage party where no one spoke English, but many drunk-sounding witnesses swear they saw a young kid, seventeen, maybe eighteen stab himself in the chest with a butcher's knife, right through the heart, reportedly saying to his older brother, 'You'd rather I was dead, wouldn't you!' Then immediately fell dead. Reportedly—and how sad."

"On our way!" Mick replied and they headed back to Lawler's unmarked and unremarkable sedan. The only plus to the car was the free use and mileage reimbursement. At the scene, it appeared the party was over in a flash, coolers filled with beer and whiskey and Tequilla left in the lurch. Only two young people kneeled over the body, face up, the knife still protruding stake like. Mick quickly ascertained that the crying pair were a girlfriend and a boyfriend, and that Jose Hernández swung both ways, a possible reason that big brother, Diego had, according to the tearful friends, who'd witnessed the suicide, had urged Jose to kill himself.

"This one's sure to be a case for the detectives and the prosecutors, Joe," Mick suggested. "We go to the residence, arrest big brother, take him in, one-and-done."

"I got no problem with that. Damned disturbing how a kid's life is gone in a flash because he's born a certain way, and why should it matter to anyone else if the kid's gender ID doesn't in any way threaten any damn one."

"One of the great mysteries of our modern-day existence, I reckon."

"Daisy's going to shed some tears over this, I'm sure."

"So too the family; one child dead, another possibly going away for encouraging his brother's suicide."

***

Joseph Wambaugh, cop author seldom to never got policing wrong, not in his TV scripts for *Police Story* or his novels such as *The Blue Knight* or *The Onion Field*. Vegas' Onion Field was more a Cactus Field just west of the lights, and once a new guy was accepted by the local officers, he was okay to join the off-duty crowd in the desert where stories told proved to slip out with heavy-duty drinking. The darkest of the dark stories were swapped. The darker or more comedic, the better.

With Mick's having cleared Lawler's way, vouching for Joe, after a few beers and an hour's coaxing, he was ready to tell a tale he'd long hoped to clear from his memory. With that introduction he began around the fire, saying, "Midwest suicide where the 'Jubilation T. Cornpone' type politician, elected County Coroner—not an investigator, and not an M.E. mind you, no Medical Examiner training, arrives while State Police E.T. evidence tech and I were still processing the scene of an apparent suicide, but possible staged murder."

"Seems Joe's curse," Mick put in.

Lawler ignored Mick and continued. "Young drunk man's wife had left him in their small Cape Cod home, taking their children, and he's by now's spent a year drinking, and in a funk, deep depression. He'd put a long barrel .20-gauge pump shotgun under his chin while lying on a stained plaid couch, one ankle over the armrest, the other on the floor. The dirty white sock on his right foot still has a deep indentation in the sock between big toe and second toe, where he's stuck his toe into the trigger guard and has apparently pulled the shotgun trigger with his toe. The shotgun's still under his chin, no apparent wound there at first, and his tongue is sticking out of his mouth, black, swollen, and looking for all the world like someone's shoved a black rubber racquetball between his lips and into his teeth. Creepy as it sounds, his eyes are open and there's lots of hard liquor and beer on the floor and coffee table next to the couch.

So far, Joe's story has elicited a chorus of *uhhs* and *ahhs*, but not much more than that. He carried on with the true tale, adding, "Checked his eyes with the finger tap to eyeball method, but no pulse. Despite this the arriving *para-magicians*, okay, paramedics, they insist that we remove the shotgun, or they'd remove it and toss it in a corner; this much to the chagrin of the salty fifteen-year veteran state police evidence tech who'd years before laterally transitioned to E.T."

"Go on," encouraged a cop that Joe only knew as Banner.

"Well, this old veteran, with gloved hands, he carefully removed the decedent's hands from the shotgun barrel, and he set it on a kitchen counter atop of the fleece lined and open unzipped rifle case it had likely been removed from."

"Then what?" asked an inebriated Mick.

"Then we see an oddly sealed wound like a quarter coin size puncture under the decedent's chin. Oddly, there was no other blood, and the top of his head was uncharacteristically, *not* blown off."

"What's the point of this story?" asked another drunken cop.

"Within moments of arriving, the paramedics opened the dead man's snap plaid shirt and put EEG electrodes on his chest, and they ran a tape which showed no sign of heart activity or life. I swear they were poised to start

CPR on the corpse immediately if there'd been any sign at all."

"They need the practice or what?" Mick joked.

"Point is, in Illinois, the paramedics often do CPR on a corpse all the way to ER, where an ER doctor will pronounce a rather delayed time of death. They don't trust us, don't even trust the paramedics to pronounce in the field."

"That's it? That's your story?" asked Banner.

"That's it, and I'm sticking to it, yeah." By this time Lawler had a buzz on.

Mick tried to help punch up Joe's story. "In Las Vegas, pronouncing and time of death, cause and manner of death, are the purview of the assigned coroner's investigator, and the paramedics will leave the body for the coroner, or stop an ambulance truck on the side of the road in route, to wait for a coroner's investigator."

"In this case, our case, the guy was flatline, and it was a crime scene which was police jurisdiction in Illinois, so the paramedics cleared the call. Myself and E.T. continued to process the scene in peace. No suicide note and when E.T. carefully racked the slide on the shotgun, we found that the brass and yellow plastic .20 gauge freshly fired shotgun shell, which along with the lower part of the barrel by the receiver. Twilight Zone time when I saw that the shell was completely filled with pink-gray liver paste. Or rather brain splatter. The light .20-gauge birdshot, instead of blowing the top of his head off, had bounced around his brain pan, and the pureed brains had dripped down the barrel and filled the shotgun shell. The E.T. carefully placed the shell *open-end-up* on a paper towel next to other collected evidence items. You know, scrapings from under the decedent's fingernails, Q-tips, cotton swabs, developing Polaroid instamatic photos, and such on the kitchen counter next to the rifle. The shell was carefully placed, *open end up*, like I said, to be sealed with brain matter intact, packaged, bagged and marked."

Joe Lawler had everyone's attention by now, and without interruption, he went on to say, "As we continued to process the scene, a single female coroner employee arrived to remove the body to take it into the county seat for autopsy. Sound familiar, Mick? Testing ladies coming into the field seems a universal trademark of the coroner's office from Chicago to Vegas."

Things fell silent around the desert campfire, as it seemed there was no more tales to tell, so Lawler went on about how things went down in Illinois "…the Coroner's employees removed the bodies, and held for autopsy, or to be claimed by family and their selected funeral homes."

Mick picked it up from there, saying, "Here, funeral homes work in rotations under the coroner's jurisdiction, and they remove the body to the Coroner's Office, the morgue for autopsy, or to their own facilities, hoping the next of *kin'll* choose them for the funeral arrangements, since it is already there, I mean if they did not have other prior relationship or arrangement."

"Hold on, Mick, you didn't let me finish the good part of the story," Lawler complained. About Then the tubby elected county coroner, a cross mix of Colonel Tom Parker, Colonel Harlan Sanders and Jubilation T. Cornpone, you know, from the Little Abner comics? The1959 movie? Anyhow, he arrives on scene, finally… Fact is, we'd never once seen him in the field or out on a call before. The man was a pure politician with no particular skills, medico-legal training. He'd been our Lake County Coroner for as long as I could remember. And he was re-elected again and again because he was a popular local figure."

"Seen a lot of that bullshit, too," added Mick, slurring his words now.

"He took a lot of information from us for *his* report. I couldn't understand why he was out in the field on a call. The County Sheriff doesn't go out on patrol with his deputies, nor the elected Coroner out with his assistant Coroners in Illinois, but here he was. Maybe the suicide's family had clout. To this day, who knows. He or she, they were department heads, administrators, and rarely did any work of the profession beyond press conferences, ribbon cuttings, kissing assess, as well as babies, speechifying, and hiding in offices behind big expensive desks."

Guess we all have that in common too, *eh* Lawler?" asked Banner, warming to Joe's story.

"Seen a lot of that bullshit, too," added Mick, slurring his words now.

"Just couldn't understand why he was there. County Sheriff', their deputy guys as well as squad cars on traffic and patrol you expect to see, same with assistant coroners, but not so much as a chief coroner. He or she, they were administrators, like I said." Pausing to sip his *Heineken*, Lawler resumed. "But for some reason, the County Coroner was here on this scene at 01:30 a.m. And after getting what he needed from us, this glad-handing relic began cleaning up the crime scene! Even as we continued to finish processing, bagging and tagging. I mean what the fuck? It was a good thing we had already sketched and taken death scene photos. The coroner found sponges, rags, spray disinfectant and cleaning bottles, as well as large black plastic trash bags, and began cleaning the place. To me it was *surreal*. I whispered a question to the State Police E.T. about it, and he just raised his eyebrows and shrugged. The County Coroner was above both our pay grades."

"So what happened next?" asked a high-school-faced rookie as he raised his beer high.

"The coroner collected all the beer cans and liquor bottles, put dirty dishes in the sink, threw out any fast-food containers and debris, emptied and wiped ashtrays clean, wiped off the kitchen counter, wiping around our marked bags and small, sealed evidence boxes. Generally fucking up the crime scene. Surreal, really!"

"Jesus," muttered Bonner, "and the ET's just let this go?"

"What could they do? Forfeit their jobs?" Lawler shrugged and went on, saying, "Next thing ya know the man flipped over a couple of brain-stained couch cushions and a throw pillow, so the stains were on the bottom or backside to be unseen? He did the same for a urine-stained couch cushion in the middle. All I could think was that these messy spots might be unseen, but they'd certainly and soon start smelling of decomposing body fluids. In short order."

"What the hell *kinna* stupid is that?" asked another of the surrounding cops.

"Apparently, the coroner wasn't too concerned as if he knew that this time around that death scene cleaners had been hired, more rare than the families, once allowed back into a scene, would find it really as exactly as left as is, left for further processors and investigators to have a final look-see."

"That is damn weird," said Mick, on his butt now, leaning against someone's squad car.

"Then he took all the trash bags out and to the curb. We had no idea when the next trash pickup day was, but we felt somewhat relieved when he gave us his business card, said we'd be advised when the inquest would be, and then he departed."

"Just leaving you guys as if knowing you couldn't say fucking word, *eh*?" asked a sergeant who had remained silent until now.

"Again, it was surreal and not SOP or routine, that much for sure."

Instead of SOP, more like SNAFU," Mick managed to get out.

Lawler went back to his now most engaging part of his story: "But the *pièce de resistance* was that after we carried everything out to the back of the E.T.s State issued S.U.V. and began to re-check and inventory, we double checked the scene and locked the door after us, we could not find a box with a sealed shotgun shell full of brains.

We double and triple checked, and ended up using some flexible tools the E.T. had to break back into the house and looked around. For the life of us, we could not find the damned brain-filled shotgun shell.

We checked under furniture, likely cabinets, between the cushions. We were stumped but could not leave without this crucial evidentiary piece of this incident.

We found a white medium sized old plastic rubbish can under the sink, full of a lot of paper towels that the coroner had used to clean the scene. And there in the middle, top up without spilling out the brains, was the shotgun shell. The coroner had seen it sitting on the paper towel on the counter and had swept it up along with the other soiled paper towels and debris, before the E.T. had had a chance to seal the top, bag and tag it. Amazingly, the brains hadn't spilled out. We completed our task, exited, and relocked the door on our way out."

Mick said from his sitting position, "Pretty obvious that your coroner guy was following someone's orders to clean up a suicide for reasons unknown. Pretty damned unethical, to say the least."

"No, you don't get it, Mick. It was a homicide made to look like a suicide, but the hitman had done a dumb ass job of it."

All the others toasted to Joe's assessment of the Illinois situation that he'd had to deal with, and some asked, "Did you ever learn of the suicide's connections…I mean homicide's connection. Was it to the mob, or the legislature, or the court?

"Would you believe all three? An attorney in too deep to all three."

On their way back to Vegas and their homes, with Joe driving, Mick, pretty much out of it, Joe asked, "So. what was the final chapter to your storrryyy baak thar, Joe?"

"Hell, long months later at the County Courthouse, the Coroner's inquest…jury was made up of senior and octogenarians who had not made it from the jury pool onto any other court hearing that day. We were in a back conference room with a whiteboard and long oval table. I wasn't too familiar with inquests at the time and was surprised how much the coroner led and explained things to the jurors, steering them to the *correct* conclusion," began Lawler.

"Oh, that it wasn't a suicide, but a homicide?"

"No that it was not a homicide but a suicide."

"Really?"

"By this time, I figured they—*whoever they were*—had seriously threatened the man's family.

"Copy that."

"One juror kept insisting that it must be a homicide, because I had testified that it was a long barrel shotgun, and with the end of the barrel under his chin, the decedent could not have reached the trigger with his fingers."

"Grant, the coroner had to keep explaining repeatedly, that I had also testified and shown photos that the decedent's sock was indented between his big and second toes, right next to the trigger, as if he had pressed the toes and sock through the trigger guard to pull the trigger with his toe."

"So, in the end?"

"Yeah, they returned the best most likely ruling—a suicide. Partially on my testimony."

"Not your doing, buddy."

"Bothers me still."

TEN

421, another scene of death

Hangover or not, the following day by four, Lawler got a call from Mick to pick him up for a scene that every cop in the greater Las Vegas area wanted to see.

"What's it all about, Mick?"

"Tell *ya* when we're on the road."

"Why don't you get your car from the cactus field? I still have to check in with HQ."

"Fuck that. My car's been towed—repossessed. Just get over here. I don't want to arrive at a scene in an Uber car."

"This scene must be something big or damned disgusting."

"Count on it. Get here, buddy."

"It wasn't lost on Joe that this was the second time that Mick had called him buddy, a word he used infrequently for others. "Be right there, Mick, buddy."

"Don't waste time with shaving or buttoning up your uniform. On the double. No coffee or donut stops."

***

Lawler sped for Mick's place, breaking a few laws even with his single strobe light atop his unmarked police vehicle. Once he saw Mick pacing outside, he pulled to a stop and Mick hastily got in, giving Joe directions to a train track location.

"What's this all about, Mick?"

"Just drive. Hit your strobe. Go!"

Once Joe got underway, Mick explained the rush. Want to get to the scene before the ET guys bag this guy's head. Least I think it's a guy. Mueller said hobo. Severed head is all I know."

"For real, seriously, this is what you got me speeding all over Vegas for?"

"Just get us there. It's not every day we get a case that's not old guy does himself in, Joe. Jurisdiction is questionable, so it might still be up for grabs."

Once at the scene, it appeared every day and night shift cop, many who'd been at the Cactus Field the night before were on hand at the semi-residential area buttressed against the train tracks, an area that sought the award for being as far away as any local area appeared from looking like the Vegas strip. *A truly hardscrabble underbelly of a place,* Joe thought.

On joining the other cops, a palpable buzz of interest mixed with curiosity and theory-hammering seemed at work here, and the only silent men were the busy ETs processing the scene. The cop that had called Mick,

Mueller, rushed to Mick and Joe to say, "I got the ETs to wait on you, Mick. The head's still where it was found by a lady walking her dog out here."

"Take us to it, John," replied Mick.

Mueller did so, and the sight was enough to turn Lawler's empty stomach. He turned away only to see the rest of the hairy, bearded man's body lying at the train tracks. Mueller noticed Joe's reaction and said something that had been repeated by others: "Musta needed a shave." And another said, "A haircut, I think." These remarks, causing laughter in some standing about, Joe saw the reason why, as the body laid adjacent to the train track, *headfirst*, but the head sent spinning away like a soccer ball.

Again, the question invaded everyone's mind: *suicide*? Or had the guy used the rail as a pillow to support his neck, possibly too drunk to hear the train coming, or as Joe imagined, put further into the Land of Nod by the vibration of the oncoming train that killed him. Joe imagined that it was most likely no one aboard the train, not a conductor, not the engineer, nor a passenger had seen the man's head cascade away, the head taken off in a split moment of time by a slow-moving train wending its way through Tinsel Town. The Coroner's Investigator had finished his examination. And the funeral van drivers were struggling to get their gurney over stone and weeds and up the hill to their van.

For reasons, Joe couldn't fathom for now, everyone had stood back and stood by to leave this death scene for Mick to investigate; Joe overheard mumblings about

Mick having shown up at a police-only Halloween party with a brutally lifelike woman's head, holding the thing by her long blonde tresses. He'd had it made up by some filmmaker makeup professional he knew, and it could not be more realistic than John the Baptist's head on a platter. Thus, was born "Mick the Trick".

Here the dead man was easy to ID, as he had as head matched a Nevada ID card. While not a driver's license, the ID card sported his picture. Mick bagged money in his wallet, too, saying, "*Prob'ly* leftover from Social Security."

"Nice pair of jeans," Lawler said to Mick, referring to what the deceased was wearing. Mick had the ETs bag the head, and he'd joined Joe at the rest of the dead man. "Neck severed like a grocery butcher slices a ham. Hardly any blood."

"Why'd they call him a hobo, Mick?" Lawler asked.

Old torn plaid shirt and the location. Possibly came in on a freight train. As for the jeans…"

Mick pointed to a small coroner's property bag left near where the head had been found. Visible through the clear plastic: a pack of Marlboros, a Hershey bar and two receipts. "The nice jeans, courtesy of and cheap at the Salvation Army."

"Didn't know they had such good clothes at the SA."

"Estate sales. Great stuff, if you don't mind wearing a dead man's clothes. If you're not, you know, superstitious."

"Didn't do our guy here any precious good."

"Had a vest from SA once; swear it was damned haunted. Shit happened to me every damn time I wore that thing."

The funeral van drivers placed the corpse in the body bag, and the Coroner snuggled the head in with torso to assure it wouldn't bang and roll around on the drive to the CCCO Coroner's Office.

"Reunited." Mick said to the accompaniment of a train whistle in the distance.

ELEVEN

10-23: at location indicated.

Dr. Jessica Coran pulled back the sheet from a middle-aged male Caucasian man. Balding. Some burgundy and purple lividity pooling a couple inches up from where he lay on his back. She'd decided that her students were by now ready for what she called "Cement Sarcophagus Man," adding, "Make a great movie monster if we could figure a way to get him up and moving."

"Still too big for any wheeled gurney," Lawler observed, tapping the slab the big corpse had been laid out on by two of Coran's assistants. Portions of stone mixed concrete crumbled inward about the head, desert dirt, and still living spiders climbed in and out of the hole in his forehead.

"I would've thought the spiders might've froze to death in the cooler," Joe observed.

"They hibernate well," Coran assured him.

"Any ID go with him?" asked Loudin.

"Afraid not."

"Found you said in that vast desert out there, but…" began Loudin, "however was he found—and are you sure *he is ahh a he*?"

Coran smiled and said, "We did a little chipping away. As to how he was discovered among the cacti, interesting story. Literally, shit luck. When a tourist's dog really had *to go* and near little town of Blue Diamond, Calico Basi."

"Stupid to do the burial on a tourist loop," said Fred.

"Most criminals are not masterminds," replied Lawler.

Coran continued. "Anyhow, this family, they let Rover out right at the spot where he could easily alert on the decomp odor. Alerted on a small gopher-sized sink hole in the ground and he began digging and wouldn't stop. The tourist tried pulling Rover away when they smelled the decomp and saw the cement sarcophagus head buried in the desert. At first, they thought they had a valuable archeological find, but as Rover uncovered more, and the stench rose, they decided to call 9-11 rather than the local university archeologist guys, like our infamous Abraham Stroud."

"Must've been a shock to the family," replied Loudin.

"And a disappointment, I imagine." Lawler shrugged. "Not a big money discovery after all."

"Wasn't long before Sac man here was totally exposed for what he was. Mixed bag, a regular motley crew came from every *g'damn* jurisdiction; I mean everyone rushed to the spot when word got out that a 'mummy was discovered in the desert'. Despite all the official vehicles surrounding Rover's discovery, not even our coroner's

RV was large enough to fit this big, *concreted*, poor devil for transport."

Lawler said, "So, someone or *two* had taken bags and bags of concrete, a large amount of water, and the means of mixing it all out to the desert, to bury and cover the man, turning him into this *mummy*, but uneven mixing…"

"Caused part of the cement over his head to cave in?" Loudin finished Joe's question for him.

Nodding, Dr. Coran said, "Thus, allowing odor out, and serendipity and Rover did the rest."

"Imagine the ride back to here was a rattling one," added Fred.

"Wouldn't fit in funeral van. Had to flatbed the sarcophagus back to the morgue for exam. Flapping tarp. Looked like a body or sarcophagus on the highway. Caused a lot of curiosity, especially with long-haul truckers. Back at the Coroner's Office, we learned that *Mummy Man* was covered in spiders and other decomp bugs coming out of the hole in his head. Creatures had moved into their new digs, so to speak."

"Nestled right in," Fred unnecessarily added.

One student asked, "Who calls their dog Rover anymore?"

"Australians," Dr. Coran replied without missing a beat.

"Was Rover the dog's real name or…?" this from Loudin.

"I use Rover for all dogs that figure in forensic cases. You'd be surprised how much evidence clues are brought to us from dogs, so I can't recall all their names. Like the little scraper that took off with a dead man's hat then decided to return it full of his DNA but also the killer's."

Regardless of what Chief Lewis had ordered, and what Mick had told Joe Lawler he shouldn't do, he couldn't step away from his own gut feeling that at least some of the so-called suicides that others had so quickly and nonchalantly written off as just that might warrant further investigation… To that end, he had begun, on his own time, look more thoroughly into the deaths he had questions roiling within his gut, his mind, and his soul. One key question he wished to see in the photo evidence which he was looking over at the moment was the common gray duct tape that had bound the two male lovers' hands to one another. The more he stared at the taped hands with the two dangling bodies in the double autoerotic deaths, the more he felt the questions bubbling in his head. He'd asked the new guy at the crime lab to run the duct tape for DNA and compare what he found to that of the dead men, but returning for answers, young Noah confessed he'd had more pressing work handed him by his superiors.

Pissed, Lawler now took an iPhone photo of the hand-holding evidence, and unbeknownst to the cage guard, he sneaked the bag with the tape out of the evidence area with a plan in mind.

Perhaps he could interest Dr. Coran in his curious investigation. After her long years of successfully bringing home serial killers and murderers who thought they'd pulled off the perfect crime, who better to rope into Lawler's curious probe? A probe into what everyone else had chalked up as a double suicide of two old gay guys who followed through on a double death pact. Had it coming, a longtime coming, love is murder…and the more cops had come in for a look-see, the more the judgments had come, while Lawler had felt he'd best choke on his judgement. The one he wished to share with Coran who had access to the lab and the microscopes.

Later that night in class

Joe waited for the first snack and cigarette break in the class to approach Dr. Coran with first the iPhone photo of the lovers' hands, explaining the unusual circumstances of the double autoerotic deaths of the two men.

"Unusual" she agreed.

"And the taped together hands. How's that possible? One would have to be on his feet to do that and then with one hand *strapped*, he'd then climb into his harness?"

She gave this thought. 'I see what you're saying, but these men may've worked it somehow…I know not how, but then have you seen some of the gymnastic acts on *America's Got Talent*?"

"Can you please do me one favor surrounding this suicide pact?"

"We-well," she stuttered, adding, "I suppose if it's within the possible. What is it?"

He pulled the brown bag from his blazer pocket.

"You brought a lunch?"

"Inside. No tuna fish sandwich."

"What then?"

"The duct tape that held the two victims' hands together," he confessed.

"You lifted it from evidence lockup? And you want me to be an accessory to your crime? Joe, I don't know you that well, now do I? And you're asking a *helluva* favor, one that could cost me and you our jobs."

"But what if my theory is right?"

"But what if you're wrong?"

Then I'm wrong, but I can say I did my damned best."

"What do others who've been to the scene say about it, Joe?" Her voice spoke of her skepticism and reluctance."

"I've read some of your case files in the journals; they always told me you were fearless and independent. Maybe I've come to the wrong person, Dr. Coran."

Other students began drifting back into the classroom. A few of the more observant felt that something was going on between Joe and the teacher. Coran lightly said to Lawler, "Leave the bagged tape on my desk, and pass your cell phone photo to my phone ASAP."

Joe took this as a good sign, so he did as told. As soon as all her students had returned from the smoke break, Dr. Coran took what seemed a pause to check her texts messages, when in fact, finding the photo of the duct-taped hand holding, she plugged her phone into a newly minted classroom device that sent the image onto a white board for all to see and study. She then reminded everyone of a truth about her class that all had heard repeatedly: "What happens in this class, stays in this class."

She then announced that, "We're going into another depth of death investigation. One I am sure you all had hoped to've seen sooner in this class—the actual *investigation* part of death investigation, that is when cause of death is in *question*." She then unhesitatingly laid out Lawler's case, telling the class that while a hypothetical case, that it was based on actual events in Las Vegas.

"We will *ream* this case wide open, working in teams of two. So, choose a partner for now. As the students milled about, seeking a partner, Loudin and Lawler quickly found one another coupling up. As the others awkwardly coupled up, Coran, using gloved hands and tweezers, lifted the duct tape from the brown paper bag, explaining why paper rather than plastic proved of better use in collecting and storing evidence. She finished with, "While not a contest to pit you all against one another, the first team to return with what the LA County PD arrived at to compare that is as Coroner Telgenoff arrived at—not necessarily the same conclusions—well, I will treat that team to a meal at the *Strat*. How y'all feel about that?"

Clapping and whistles followed, as the Stratosphere was among the best eateries in Vegas. It had only recently rebranded itself as *the Strat*.

The teams were told that since it was a theoretical case that any theoretical use of police tools and police science could be used. *The game was afoot.* But for Lawler and Dr. Jessica Coran, this was hardly a game or a classroom assignment.

Class over, everyone sent on a scavenger hunt of sorts to ply their imaginations over the slight evidence in their theoretical case, Lawler, who'd had great respect for Dr. Coran M.E., now held great respect for Dr. Coran as a medico-legal professor. She'd not only put the 'kids' to work on Joe's theory of the crime, but she'd also create *plausible deniability* for herself. *Smart*, should her lesson, her accessory to Joe's crime, and actual evidence having found its way into her hands—into her classroom, it could be hell to pay. It was the risk she took: should the facts break out from her classroom.

TWELVE

911 – Exigent circumstances; caller in immediate danger.

As it turned out, the Rattler was an on old and tired trick that Mick used often to get laughs from his fellows in the prime directive: 'do no harm' and when possible, have a good laugh at the expense of the new guy or the rookies. Getting a good one over on the new guy who'd signed on to the healthy if not always possible idea painted on the LA cruisers: *to serve and protect.*

"So, the Rattler's your jalopy, eh, Mick, and you let me suffer through for a damn week and a half!"

"Well hell, *you* being a savvy old dog, Joe, I thought *you'd've* caught on by…well, a lot sooner. Who blew it?"

"A guy in my night class named Fred. Seems he drove the Rattler before me."

"Ol' Red Fred, sure."

"Good guy, Fred. Two years he's retired. Taking the class anyway."

"Fred's okay, but he talks too much."

How's that?"

"Told me a little story about how somehow you and your prof concocted an assignment around the double-suicide case we put away."

"Did, did he?"

"Lawler, Joe, if this so-called assignment were to find its way to the ears of the brass, it could hurt everyone in that class, including you, that young girl you have your eye on, your prof, all of them, but mostly you."

"Then I'll take full responsibility."

"Noble of you, pal. But sounds to me you've turned 'em all into accessories after the fact. And what about me?"

"What about you, Mick?"

"I'm your unofficial training officer, Joe! You think they won't think me involved in this? Really?"

"Hadn't given my steps enough forethought, I reckon now. But be assured, pal, I'd vouch you had nothing to do with my taking a bag of tape out of lockup."

"By then who's left to believe you, Joe. Your hold on reality, man, I'm beginning to question."

"And yours? How long did it take you to get under the dash and remove every nut and bolt to create the Rattler?"

Mick defended this with, "No more time than our fellow Blue Knights are spending on their damned iPhones these days."

"Kills me to see so many citizens walking the streets of Vegas of all places like zombies with their phones, walking into deadly traffic."

"Sure, Joe, change the subject. You're good at that." Mick looked agitated, trying to steady the awful monster noise of his creation by placing both hands on the dashboard in a failing attempt to control the noise even if a little."

"What about giving the double suicide another look, partner? What if we throw our combined weight against the idea of its being 'just another old guy suicide'? What might come of a real investigation?" Lawler knew that he had to somehow get Mick to believe such a change in his view of the crime had to be his notion and not just Joe's alone. "I need your help, Mick. You know the terrain and the players."

"That's the truth."

"The street walkers, the hierarchy of sex workers, from the classy 'massage' ladies to the casino cougars, to the cheaper corner girls. You know all the hotel workers from the desk clerks, the bellhops and janitorial and maid staff to the pit bulls in the casino, the cooks and wait—"

"Enough, enough…Ok already with the compliments."

"Does that mean you're willing to invest some shoe leather with me? Ask questions?"

Lawler flashed an iPhone photo he'd taken of the two men who'd died with hands taped together and thus, without *spotting* one another—names Henri Jorgensen and Marti Wynne."

"We can ask around if they'd been seen in the company of one or more men or perhaps partying with women on the night they died."

THIRTEEN

10-13 Déjà vu all over again.
The unwanted unwarranted recurring dream…

Lawler woke up clutching the rumpled sheets and light blanket. He had hit his head on the dark wooden headboard because sometime during the night his pillows had been pushed off the bed and onto the floor.

He had dreamt *that* dream again. The one that started with him being dumped into a hole in the desert, and poorly mixed concrete being poured over and around him from the back of a pickup truck, just like the Mummy Man, "John Cement Doe," aka Cement Sarcophagus Guy, who was chilling back in the cooler at the morgue. Only in this recurring dream it was Lawler who was being buried in the desert, in a concrete tomb.

His first thoughts were *"Oh no, Déjà vu all over again"* for this familiar scene. Then the wet poorly mixed concrete filled his mouth, his ears, and then he dare not open his eyes, keeping them tightly squeezed shut as the muck rose over them, encasing his entire body.

Then, having omniscient dream vision, he saw two stock image gangsters with indeterminate faces shoveling desert hard-pan and small pieces of caliche back over the top of the concrete. Then they drove the truck over it a few times to pack it down before driving away toward the city lights. Leaving him I their wake, leaving him paralyzed, trapped beneath the red earth. Leaving him to be the largest Egyptian sarcophagus ever seen in a museum or on the History Channel.

It struck him that this might well be a dream. He tried to wake up, to move, to get up out of bed, but he couldn't move. He began to see himself both laying in the desert tomb, and simultaneously tightly wrapped 'mummy-fashion' in his bed covers. It was like he'd read about: sleep paralysis, for even screaming the silent scream, he could not wake himself from this prison of paralysis. Until a sudden full bladder woke him with an urgency. He disentangled himself from the covers and hurried through the bathroom door.

FOURTEEN

10-13 Déjà vu again.
The penultimate dream…

The dream started as it had before. Only this time, from the omniscient view of his dream state, Lawler could hear the world above him changing. The desert was being landscaped and paved over as the rapidly spreading city and suburbs sprawled further and further into the desert. He heard the construction of houses and businesses and saw the structures taking form in a *workie-jerky* fast motion scene like a movie montage. Then he heard, before he felt pressure from above as a giant asphalt roller formed and pressed a huge parking lot onto the desert hardpan above his cement tomb.

Then he felt something below him. He wasn't alone in this cement slab sarcophagus. Hoarse cries and rough whispers assaulted his ears. He could feel a damp, moldy breath on the back of his neck as shredded clawing hands and nails tore at his bloody back and shoulders–somehow inside the cement with him.

Terrified he strained upward, away from the pain. Suddenly there was some space around him and above him. Not enough to stave off the claustrophobia, but enough to claw the rough scrabble stone and rock concrete mix above him, bloodying his fingers and shredding and pulling out his fingernails—even as the decaying mummy man below him was clawing apart his back.

Get out! Get Away! Get out! He kept clawing and clawing. Surely the mummy man would kill him, if he wasn't dead already, suffocated, trapped, and dead, dead, dead.

But then, cement dust and rock fell on his face, and he coughed as he choked it in, trying again to breath. There came open a small hole. Then desert sand poured in on him, and above that, a smaller hole, through which he could see blue lot lights and a dark starry sky. Faint, then stronger, he reached his fingers up through the small, short tunnel-like holes, pulling stone, sand, and bits of asphalt into the tomb, big enough so he could push his head upward and through to air to breathe deeply in.

Somehow, he wriggled through that small head-sized hole in the parking lot above, and he stepped one foot out, but he still had one foot trapped several feet below in the hole. He pulled but was grasped and held fast by the rook-like claws of Mummy Man.

He stepped, he tugged, he pulled, but he could not free his leg. Then he started to step up and out onto the asphalt parking lot. Free! It was nighttime. The blue LED parking lot lights cast a soft glow in the night. The suburbs and the city had sprung up around this parking lot and in the distance, all of Vegas, everything, all was a glowing blue. *Blue Vegas*, he thought. Then he woke up, again.

***

410-76, In route to Glitter Gulch.
From the Vegas Strip to downtown Fremont Street
Experience

Bill Stedman and Steven Wellmore checked into the
Palace Station Hotel and Casino having taken a shuttle
from Harry Reid Airport. Along the shuttle ride to the
Palace, Wellmore asked Stedman, "Did you know that
ex-Senator Harry Reid was the basis of Tommy
Smother's councilman character in the movie Casino?"

"No way! You sure?"

The Palace Hotel-Casino was on Sahara Avenue, just
across highway I-15 from the Las Vegas Strip.

"Can we get the "*O.J. room?*" Stedman asked the desk
clerk, a cute college age professional with a Debbie
Reynolds haircut, whose name badge said "Tarron" over
the italicized "Idaho." Stedman slid a $20 bill across the
counter.

"I'm sorry, sir, but I don't know what you're talking
about," Tarron said, effecting a blank stare.

"You know, the room where O.J. at gunpoint tried to
take back his old sports memorabilia from the floating
flea market. At gunpoint. OK, you're young, but it was
all over the news."

"I'm sorry."

Stedman slammed his palm over the twenty and pulled it
back. "*Humph!*"

Wellmore slid a $50 bill across the counter. Tarron starred at it for only a moment, then snatched the $50 and slipped it into a side vest pocket. "Look, you seem like a couple of nice old gents. But management doesn't want to acknowledge the incident. Not the image and branding they are looking to present. Besides, the tower that had that room was demolished two renovations ago. But I'll tell you what. Let me upgrade you to one of our top tower suites with a view of the strip. You can see the Eiffel Tower, The MSG Sphere, and the Seminole Hard Rock Hotel."

Stedman erupted, saying, "The Hard Rock Hotel! It looks like a giant neon Gibson guitar, taller than the Luxor Pyramid. We should have stayed there."

"Come on! You old coot," began Wellmore. "It's an upgrade to a suite! Don't look a gift hors' d'oeuvre' in the mouth." He pronounced it *whores-doovrah*, embarrassing the young lady at the desk.

***

After settling into their suite without unpacking, Wellmore wanted to take a nap, but Stedman talked him into heading out for a couple of drinks at *Glitter Gulch*, downtown on Fremont Street. They took the double decker *Deuce* open air bus, so they could once again soak up, revel, and take in the LED updated neon dream that was the Las Vegas Strip, on the way to downtown. It was cold, but they had already picked up a couple of loose cold beers from a residentially challenged guy, his cooler, and his Benji dog at the bus stop in front of the old Sahara. They took the scenic route, south past and U-turning around the *Famous Welcome To Las Vegas* sign, and back north up to the strip. Past the Welcome to Downtown lit double arches, with two elevated selfie stations on either side of the street, past a drug store, a famous taco stop, a couple of run-down strip clubs. And several movie set and real-world famous wedding chapels, where couples could get married by Elvis, Mr. Spock, Marilyn Monroe, take one's pick: James Dean, Marlon Brando or…

Then, after the brief foray through the dark run-down section, they emerged as if out of the spooky woods, at the bus station at the headwaters of the Fremont Street Experience, the Plaza Hotel. Fronted by the glass domed *"Oscar's" Steakhouse, Booze 'N Broads"* named and managed for the former 3-time Mayor and Casino mob mouthpiece, Oscar Goodman.

There existed no exaggeration of the carnival atmosphere of Fremont. Noise, smells, ambience. Smell of beer, ribs and hot dogs in the air, along with cigar smoke, and skunk weed experience up and down Fremont Street, filled with buskers, the homeless, cons and talented performers. Musicians, acrobats, and costumed posers. Vegas Vicki and heated screen pool on circa, Vegas Vick still there, Holograms? ABBA and KISS Hologram performers.

Several stages with club bands, lounge singers, Joan Jett impersonator, or multiples. Heart Attack Grill. Slotzilla. Neonopolis. Beefcake Men and exotic women dancing on multiple outdoor bars with flair bartenders. A poi and fire breathing act. Furry costumes. Happy drunk homeless guy with the largest of all the largest Fremont Street beers? Served in regulation football size plastic glass for $1, when finished downing it, the guy'd then bum quarters until he got enough for another. Looked like Roy Roger's sidekick, old prospector Gabby Hayes, dancing around his backpack like no one was watching and like he hadn't a care in the world. Tilting three sheets to the wind.

Dwarf sword swallowers and magicians. Contortionists, acrobats, living statues. Buskers, street performers and posers, must stand and perform within circles impressed into the Fremont Street walkway, signing up and reserving each space for an hour at a time, to prevent them flooding the walkway, and impeding the tourists on promenade.

Hunky men in assless chaps, and curvy women in black go-go boots, hot pants and midriff sports tops danced on top of several outdoor bars outside the Casinos.

One duo of ladies caught Stedman's eye, and he grabbed Wellmore to point the girls out. Wellmore gave a look at the pair of costumed women who somehow stood out among the multiple pairs of topless show girls with pasties and their taught asses hanging out of thongs, among the superheroes: Spiderman, the Hulk, Superman, the Iron Man and more, Elvis impersonators from all stages of his career, Lamet coated in chinos and loafers, to white sequined jumpsuits, Blonde Marilyn Monroes, Pink-attired Barbie Dolls of every size, shape, and color, pin up girls from the 50s films, and KISS impersonators, even a washed out, bland band dressed as

Tela Tubbies.

Maureen and Tammy didn't have much time left on their reservation of this prime busker's circle, and ramped their *hootchie-coo* pantomime Ballie dances up a notch or two, to entice and draw in some seriously interested tourists; bring 'em closer for a good look-see before *shift over*.

Statler wandered over to the buskers circle where a tall woman in a stitched together, shiny black vinyl Cat Woman suit, like Michelle Pfeiffer's in the Tim Burton Batman movie, stood cracking her whip up, down, and lassoing it around to draw in the punters. She vogued and posed, stretching cat-like to showcase her Amazonian figure.

Next to her, stood a tired, skinny girl with a gymnast's body and bared triple C breasts. The only thing covering her wane breasts, body paint and little circle pasties over the nipples. She had a shear Wicked Weasel string thong panty covering her clearly shaved nethers. She was body painted with just enough red and black diamonds to approximate a harlequin costume and wore a Harley Quinn hat and mask like the popular comic and movie character. She didn't say much, she just shook her tits and wiggled her hips to the *loud-loud* music. She looked entranced, deeply under the effects of Chromophile or more.

Seeing the two old geezers' frozen gaze, the shiny cat woman stepped out of the busker's circle and approached Stedman and Wellmore.

"I am the Lady-Cat Mistress C," She flicked her arm and wrist and cracked her leather knot tipped bullwhip, sounding like a shot and echoing under the Fremont Experience canopy. But between the four music stages, and cacophony of tourist drinking dancing, yelling and laughing, no one beyond Stedman and Wellmore took much notice. "And this is my partner, Harley." Harley blew a kiss and jiggled at the two aging party guys. Maureen and Tammy new better than to ever give punters, or anyone they didn't know well, their real names.

Cat said in a cat's purring voice, "How about a picture with us? Cool souvenir to show off back at your bridge club." Cat then leaned in and whispered suggestions in Stedman's ear while stroking his neck and earlobe with her nails. "You can feel up my tits and ass." She finished with her tongue in his ear.

"Geezus," said Stedman, wiping his inner ear with a handkerchief.

"How much?" asked Wellmore.

"Normally, we charge $40 dollars for a couple of pictures with us. But ya'll look like fun folks. I'll tell you what. How about $100 for two or three minutes, and you can take all the cell phone pictures you want?"

Stedman went for his wallet. Wellmore grabbed his wrist, halting him. "That's ludicrous."

Just then, there was a loud amplified sound of a slot machine jackpot alarm, coins clinking into the trough, as the giant Slotzilla slot machine 77 feet above them, opened its topmost reels, and four tourist flew over top them on ziplines, arms forward, flying like Superman, speeding all the way from one end of the canopy to the other.

Then the Casinos and businesses front lights all dimmed. The amplification on the four band stages was cut off, and there came a roar of Air Force Thunderbirds streaking across the Fremont Light Show canopy which sprung to life in blindingly bright colors, from one end, starting at the Plaza, to the faraway end at *Neonopolis* and the Fremont East Hipster tavern district at the other.

The light show on the canopy blazed like an exploding rainbow sun. First there was a loud carnival calliope version of *Viva Las Vegas* playing to images of sexy clowns and trapeze aerialist tumbling across the downtown Vegas skyline. Then Formula One race cars streaked across the canopy with another roar, wiping the carnival scenes, and playing a montage of music by KISS, Metallica and Rob Zombie. The Rob Zombie song and Munster car Dragula wiped the scene one more time, finishing with giant scenes of Pink, who soared and tumbled on high wires on the canopy to a medley of her three hardest and biggest hits.

Then the canopy went blank. And the Casino and business neon and LEDs sprung to life again, along with the amplified stage bands.

"$80." Lady-Cat counter offered, now that she could be heard.

"$50."

$70, and we won't watch the clock too closely."

Cash up front, and the ladies led the guys back into their busker's circle, which they only had reserved from the Fremont Street Association for ten more minutes. A pair of classic Vegas showgirls in red feathered headdresses with sequined bustiers and fishnets stood nearby and waiting to take over this very prime busker real estate.

First Stedman took pictures of Wellmore sandwiched between the two women. They took his hands and placed them on their tits and asses while posing, wrapping one leg around him while grinding. And Harley lifted her leg straight up in a high kick and held the pose with her boots pointed to the sky, showing that she had recently waxed all her pubic mound. Then it was Wellmore's turn to take pictures of Stedman with the women, and all the poses were repeated with little to no variation. *Practiced*, Stedman thought.

Stedman said, "Thanks." He then started to leave the circle to look at the pictures that Wellmore had taken of him in the embrace of the ladies.

"Wait a minute, stud," said the cat, as she and the other one pulled him back between them. This time around, they snuggled against him while taking his hand and putting it between their thighs, up into their pussies. Harley ground against him so much she rubbed off a substantial amount of her already minuscule body paint *costume.*

Harley crooked her little finger and Wellmore walked up to the circle, where Stedman remained blissfully sandwiched. All the while the two showgirls in red feathers looked pointedly on, then at their watches, while tapping their platform pumped boots.

"So, do you studs want to come party with Harley and me? You know, back at our room near here? You'll have the best time in Vegas guaranteed. We'll party like, I'd bet, you've never partied before."

"This isn't our normal thing," replied Wellmore.

"Fuck normal, man!" began Stedman in his friend's ear. "Come on, we'll teach these bitches a thing or two and have some laughs."

"Can we watch the two of you together?" asked Wellmore. "Maybe a threesome or a *more-some* with happy endings all around?"

"No way Jose. This whip isn't just a prop." She cracked her whip sharp and loud, turning heads and Stedman and Wellmore jumped back a step. "I'm a Dom. A *pro* Dom. Modeling and busking is just my side hustle. I don't have sex with clients. If you want a whore, go to the legal brothels in Nye County. It's only an hour and half drive. Just head out on Blue Diamond highway, then over the hump to Pahrump. The Chicken Ranch, and Sheri's Ranch Mountain Shadows Resort have the legal hookers. But those girls and staff are pirates, they'll take you for every dime they can squeeze outta your credit cards."

The cat's brief rant left the men silent. Then she added, "But, if you want to come back to our place near here, we can show you a squeezing pleasing time—for only the cost of a great night out on the town in Vegas. A good time, square deal and memories and bragging rights to last a lifetime. We even have party favors." Lady-Cat Mistress C opened a little pouch on her belt, and Stedman could see multi-colored and many-shaped pills and popper capsules.

"This *really* isn't our thing. Wellmore begged off again.

Harley, the thin short one hesitated. Wellmore creeped her out. He looked like an only slightly older version of Homer, the guy who had met her coming off the bus from Wisconsin, coming to Vegas for some adventure and a new start when she was fourteen, going on fifteen. She went from the frying pan of her awful home into the fire of the city streets. He had kept her enthralled at first but soon it turned to slavery. He used her and made her do degrading things with tourists for what seemed a lifetime. But she was a survivor. Now she was free, and Homer was buried in the desert. And for herself, she'd learned to survive on Freemont with Lady Cat, who did love and protect her. Besides, she needed the rent, and a buck was a buck.

Stedman watched her type something into her phone, and almost immediately a rickshaw, or more specifically a three-wheel electric pedal cab with fringed awning pulled around from a nearby side street and stopped in front of them. The driver was a stoned looking older man with a blunt cigar, cargo pants and a red patterned Hawaiian shirt, worn open over a stained white T-shirt.

He wore a battered and faded chauffeur cap over a greasy blond mullet and had stray locks poking out the sides. He wasn't very big, or even healthy looking, but he had bicycle thighs and pumped biceps.

Harley and Lady-Cat Mistress C ducked and climbed under the fringed Surrey canopy onto the padded bench seat. "Well guys? Going our way?"

Stedman and Wellmore looked at each other, argued a little while trying and failing to whisper, then squeezed in between the two women.

FIFTEEN

10-13 Déjà vu (all over again) but hopefully, the final nightmare.

This time from the outset, Lawler knew he was dreaming. Knowing didn't save him from the pain and fear of mental imprisonment, paralysis. He felt the weight of his body lying in his bed, gripped by his helpless state of sleep paralysis. He could not feel his body in his dream, but he was standing and watching Mummy Man, Cement Sarcophagus guy, John Cement Doe, emerge from the asphalt-like desert. First his head, then his shoulders, came breaking out, forcing their way up and out of the cement tomb, cracking and piercing the layers of his asphalt tomb here in the dream parking lot, he resurrected himself, rising through the layers. Reenacting a primal birth, he clawed, pressed, kicked and climbed and burst his way out, until he was standing across from Lawler. Glaring. Staring deep into Lawler's eyes, as if asking, "Why weren't you here to save me?"

Paralyzed both in and out of the dream state, Joe could only watch as Mummy Man approached. Step by echoing step, raising his arms toward Lawler's face before *it* pointed with arms dripping of muck and wet cement, fingers off at an oblique angle, urging Joe to look toward a nearby building. The roof, windows and door were crooked and Caligari-like. On the door, in letters burned in with orange and red charcoal embers, was a single, smoking, word, but it escaped Joe before his mind's eye could catch it as it faded away, just as he awoke in sweat and trembling nerves.

At that moment, Joe realized the recurrent dream was not about the dead man, but in his deepest subconscious, he knew the truth. It was all about him, his deepest, darkest self. And then the phone rang so loudly that it chased the prison and his conclusion straight out of his mind. He almost knocked the phone to the floor, and then he did knock it to the floor. He scrambled to locate it, half in, half out of bed, lifted it and wanted to thank whoever had awakened him from the nightmare. It proved to be Mick, saying, "Been workin' my contacts in and around the hotels, bars, casinos about two lowlife bitches who come and go."

"Is-sat right? Anything we can move on?"

"Hell no, but we can *surveil* the two. Keep eyes on'em."

"You woke me up for that?"

"What the hell, Joe? I'm out burning shoe leather, and you're snoozing?"

"Frankly, Mick, your call is a godsend."

"Nightmare again?"

"'Fraid so, yeah."

"Shit, sounds rough. Maybe 'cause of the Rattler. I'll have to put the nuts and guts back into that dash for you.

"You know, I'd appreciate that, Mick, and it might just *cement* our relationship."

"No talk of cement, my pal. Get some rest...see you later."

They hung up amicably, and Lawler went for his fridge for a drink of lemonade. He feared getting back to sleep would be damn near impossible as he somehow recalled that his subconscious had revealed that he was the victim encased in a hole in cement. He told himself that some night he meant to do a stakeout where cement man had been so foully used and to catch the man's killers. Maybe Mick could be talked into joining him in the effort. Someday.

Then he saw the crooked notepad near his bed lamp, the pen almost over the edge of the table, ready to drop, and on the pad a single 'burning' word in large letters done by a shaking hand: YOU...

Lawler eased from his bed, stood from his mattress, shook awake this time, arguing with himself that he had to shake off this damned business of the recurring drama going on in his head. How the hell could such a dream be about himself? After all, he'd never experienced such a thing as being buried alive or dead in a pit and then concreted over. The whole of it smacked of an awful Edgar Allen Poe story, like being bricked up behind a wall, but he had no cat or dog to come to his rescue, not in the dream! So, what was his subconscious trying to tell him? What did it want of him? What action was he to take anyway? Go to the pound and save a dog from the chamber? Get an animal to care for and it would take care of him? He worked on the answer even as he found a container of orange juice, poured it into a glass, and slipped in a douse of *Jack Daniels*. He swallowed in one gulp, hoping the drink might help him return to sleep, but sleep without the concrete man making another appearance in his head. He wanted to believe it was all somehow trivial, expected in his line of work, and that it did not reflect back on him. But then again, perhaps if he got a dog, then maybe the dreams would end like rising fog over a dewy field.

SIXTEEN

2-46: Unlawful Restraint. The OJ call.
That ain't the way to have fun, son. That ain't
the way to have fun...

There was just about room for a tight four passengers on
the pedal cab's seat. The women liberally draped
themselves into Stedman's and Wellmore's laps, hands
roaming. Wellmore kept checking to see that his wallet
remained in place. They were driven several blocks
through dirty side streets, refuse spinning by the cab,
and the unhoused, scrunching doglike, sleeping or
nodding below tents and sheets, others in the open on
the sidewalk.

They pulled up to the Siegel Suites, surprisingly not
related to or referencing Bugsy Siegel who was
whacked, due to skimming the mob's money when
building the Flamingo Hotel on what would become the
Vegas Strip. No, this was an aging motel chain that
rented rooms by the day or week.

"Here?" Wellmore asked, "Why didn't we…I mean, we
could've gone back to our suite at the top of Palace
Station!"

"Do you want me to hang near?" The pedal cab driver,
looking like a sometime muscle and pimp asked the cat
lady.

"No, these guys are pussycats." Eileen tipped him, and he hit the electric throttle, taking a break from peddling, and he whizzed quietly off and back to Fremont.

"What'd you call us?" Stedman asked?

"Nothing sugar." She unlocked the door to her motel room. "Home sweet home." She beckoned them inside, and Stedman flashed on a spider welcoming a fly into a web.

Both older men hesitated, peaking into the dimly lit near tenement room before following the hip swaying, sashaying women inside.

There stood a single sofa bed in the main living area, an efficiency kitchenette, and a single bathroom. Sheer fabric-colored scarves draped the two lampshades, the only two lamps in the room, one on a table next to the open sofa bed, the other on the corner floor. A worn wooden card sized dining table with four straight back wooden chairs circling it, spoke of the 'rustic' style popular ages ago.

There wasn't much deco in the room, but Wellmore noticed on the wall a colored chalk cartoon caricature portrait, obviously from the artist on Fremont in front of *Slotzilla*. In it they were bursting out from the top of Slotzilla depicted in Wonder Woman and Supergirl suits, flying in exaggerated perspective, with cartoon word balloons saying *"Wow! Whoosh! Super-friends, Maureen the Cat & Tammy Harley, ride or die!"*

Harley dragged two of the dining chairs to a front row stage distance from the open sofa bed. The two men stood hesitantly, obviously hoping for an invitation onto the bed. "Gentlemen, be seated," she said in a commanding voice that brooked no refusal.

And so, they sat.

"Harley, assume the position," ordered the cat woman.

"Yes Mistress." Harley kicked off her heels and began climbing onto the thin sofa mattress, the sheet and threadbare, gold cotton blanket with its satin trim. In exaggerated moves, as if she were performing on stage with a stripper pole, she crawled onto the bed, arching her back and rump in the air. She tumbled over onto her back still in her little round heels, and now she spread her legs in a straight, knees wide "V" with her toes pointed like a dancer's. She next spread her arms and legs over and over against the blanket, her back arched as if making a snow angel.

Maureen flipped four fleece lined red leather cuffs from under the four corners of the bed and strapped Tammy down spread eagled. She pulled a large sports bag from under the bed, and from it, she laid out various toys on the bed between Tammy's legs. Floggers, paddles, vibrators, a peacock feather, and a feather duster with a long handle. She stuffed some clean lace undergarments into Tammy's mouth, muffling her, and then set a Magic Wand vibrator lightly on its lowest setting on her pubic mound, buzzing softly. Tammy began to moan through her gag.

Maureen dismissively turned away from her 'victim',

and she pulled out two sets of black Smith & Wesson handcuffs. "I almost forgot." She walked over to the seated men. "Hands behind your back."

"Uh-Uhh!"

"No way! That wasn't part of the deal."

"It is part of the deal if I say it is. Or I keep a kill fee and you two can just up and leave. Go on, get out if you don't have the stomach for a real adventure." She smiled wickedly. "No guts no story no glory." She softly put one knee up on Stedman's crotch, rubbing rhythmically, and she reached over and squeezed Wellmore's whole package. Wellmore felt a stirring down there he hadn't felt without chemical aid in a long time. First Stedman, then Wellmore put their hands behind their backs.

"Hey Babe, take a walk on the wild side…" she sang as she handcuffed the men behind their backs, each to his respective chair.

SEVENTEEN

10-1000 (Local PD slang) Neighborhood disturbance/loud party.
I'll have what she's having.

Once the guys were secured, Lady-Cat Mistress C, returned her attention to the spread Harley, whose wriggling undulations had dislodged the Magic Wand from her crotch. She was stretching and wreathing in a vain attempt to reconnect with the vibrating toy.

"Naughty girl!" Lady Cat said and began to lightly tap Harley's pussy through the sheer thong, in a tapping spanking motion. Harley continued to moan through her cloth gag.

Mistress C went to work on her in earnest. She lightly took the black and red leather *Cat'o'nine* tails flogger and stroked it all over the younger girl's flesh, then she strappingly whipped her a few times on the thighs, raising light red streaks, far short from actual welts. The more she worked her, the more Harley wreathed and moaned. Then Cat picked up the peacock feather and traced and twirled it over all the soft spots on the girl's body, from her neck under her earlobes, armpits, abs, nether lips, back of her knees, and then stopped. Then she began tickling the girl's manacled feet and toes with the feather. Harley stopped wreathing and pulsing in ecstasy and started laughing and convulsing. Her words were muffled through the gag, but she seemed to be begging, "*Heese stot—Heese. Stot!*"

"Please stop isn't a safe word darlin'. You know that." Maueeen laughed. But she took the cloth gag out of the girl's mouth, to allow the moans to sound for the men. Next, she used the Magic Wand on the girl while massaging her front just under her thong. Harley screamed and howled like a mad woman as she climaxed. Wellmore was sure someone from motel management would come knocking on the walls or door, but no one did. They either didn't care or were used to loud bed play.

"What about us?" Stedman called out. "When's our turn?"

"Your turn for what, Pig? Aren't you enjoying the show?" She gestured at Harley on the bed, catching her breath. "You want your turn? You mean a turn with her?"

"Damn right we do!" said Wellmore who Cat began stripping down, getting halfway, feeling the man up even as he fought against his being restrained. "Feels better doesn't, young man, being cuffed, unable to touch me back? Come on tell me it ain't true, baby boy!"

EIGHTEEN

419 - Nevada Police hundred code for dead human bodies.

Murder most foul.

Lady-Cat Mistress C went into full Dominatrix mode. She ordered Harley to feel herself up from top to bottom, and to coordinate the same moves on Stedman, while she worked on Wellmore, who pissed her off more and more just by looking like her former pimp, and talking like her abusive father-in-law, both of whom had contributed more than a little to her ongoing, untreated PTSD.

The ladies now helped the cuffed men onto the bed and unbuckled the men's belts and pulled their pants and shorts down around their ankles. They next began running the feather duster over them, but now frustratingly never touching flesh to flesh.

Then Mistress C alternately grabbed Wellmore by the throat, her fingers light against the Adams apple and tightly gripping the two carotid arteries on either side, choking him, and cutting the blood flow to his brain, so he got lightheaded and when almost ready to pass out, she would let up and allow him to agonizingly gasp in air. She'd next give the other tourist a taste of dying.

"Stop it!" Stedman alternately called out in a panic, first for his friend and then for himself. "You're strangling him! You're killing me!"

"No sugar, this is just erotic breath play. Watch. Learn. Soon you'll be seeing stars and fireworks like never before."

Mistress C wrapped a thick, soft velvet rope, the kind used on stanchions at lines in banks or outside nightclubs, around Wellmore's neck, while Harley worked a flashlight between his legs, grinding it into the thighs.

"Edge him!" Dom Cat in full character shouted at Harley. "Don't let him come until he begs." And she kept alternately tightening and loosening the thick velvet rope around Wellmore's neck. With most clients, she'd have let them come by now, just to get it over with and to get rid of them. But this creep Wellmore, he really bothered her. And besides, he was still refusing to beg for release like a good boy should.

Then Wellmore caught his breath enough to speak again. "You bitch! You worthless whore!" The shouting got a reaction, as Mistress C slapped him about the face, and dumped a bucket of motel machine ice on his crotch, then the leftover, freezing water melt at the bottom of the bucket over his balding head.

"You will address me as Mistress you contemptible worm!"

"When I get loose—" Then she heard her father's voice coming out of Wellmore's mouth, as he said the last thing her father had ever said to her: "I am going to beat that whore ass of yours so hard you'll feel it in your guts for a year!"

She grabbed the velvet rope, wrapped it again around his neck and squeezed and pulled it so tight that his eyes bulged. A white-hot anger filled her, and she was oblivious to the cries from Harley and Stedman to stop. Then Maureen looked away from Harley's crying to approach Stedman, rope in hand.

NINETEEN

201.320 Living from earnings of prostitution.
Moving on up.

Maureen gave the key to Tammy and ordered her to get the handcuffs off the two dead men, Stedman and Wellmore, now just cold dead flesh, two bodies. Maureen ordered Tammy to pack up everything they owned, while she did a thorough scavenge of everything the two dead men had on them. Watches, rings, gold pinky rings, bracelets, necklaces. And in their fat wallets, an abundance of cash, travelers' checks, credit cards—And room key cards for the Palace Station.

Maureen did a last look over to make sure Tammy had gotten everything that could be connected to them packed. And then she smartly threw down a couple of a rival escort dancers' colorful, nudie biz cards.

Harley subconsciously showed one passive aggressive sign to privately disobey Cat; she'd nosily laid one set of cuffs into Cat's tool chest, but not wanting to touch any more dead flesh, she'd purposefully left cuffs on the second tourist.

"Where we *gonna* go now?" asked a shaken Harley.

"We're moving to a suite at the Palace Hotel!

***

"Wake up, Joe—believe it or not, we've got another two old guys dead in a seedy hotel, layin' in bed together the super says and possibly murdered. Shit if you've been right all along," added Mick."

"How's zat?"

"Lotta old guys *in pairs* ending it here in Vegas Valley."

"Drop by and pick me up. Can't take another hour in the Rattler."

Lawler had just finished getting dressed when Mick arrived, hitting the siren only in a blip. Joe locked his door and rushed to greet Mick and climb into the squad car and they were off.

TWENTY

10-76 In route to location.
Destination downtown, Glitter Gulch…

"What makes you think these two were murdered, Mick?"

"Night man, said one had a rope wound round the neck, so maybe. Who knows till you examine him. Why else you taking the damn night class, right?"

"Right. Figure if Lewis gets a burr in his pants and fires me, I got the death investigation to back me at another job."

"Maybe I *shoulda* taken the course with ya."

"Never too late to learn."

"Me? Take a class to determine if some dead guy's dead? Already got that gift, Joe."

Lawler belly laughed and let it go. They were soon pulling into a back street that ran like a tributary off the broad Fremont River of activity. This time it appeared no other cruisers wanted to be on hand, and Joe wondered why this was so. When he asked Mick about it, Mick hesitated before saying, "Just 'cause a man wears a blue uniform most his day and night doesn't mean he's not susceptible to these flesh peddlers, so it's like a kind of shame, especially to the married with kids fellas, so…"

"So?"

"So, they avoid the time and place like old tourist are drawn to it, opposites you might say."

"Ever think of going into the psychiatry game, Mick?"

"Cops like social workers and teachers gotta be half-shrinks, man. Especially in a place like we got here."

Mick parked the car close to the registry window almost hitting it. The night clerk ala manager rushed out to greet him, obviously knowing him by name. "It's bad, Mick. Neither of the two have a pulse."

"Norm, what caused you to check on them?" Mick took the hotel key from Norman and studied the number and started for the room in question.

"Heard a lot of noise but let it go. Can't stop folks frolicking, can't lose what little business we have here. This ain't the MGM, you know."

"That'd be my first clue, Norm. But answer my question, man."

"Should I call a bus, Mick?" Lawler interrupted.

"Hell no, Joe! Not till you roll 'em and do your homework, impress your teacher."

"OK, guess I got that coming, but no high-fives or shaking hands with the dead, alright?"

"You're on. But I know you're *fookin'* with me this time!"

"Their eyes," said Norm, the night man.

"What about their eyes?" Joe asked.

"They were, both of them, bug-eyed, staring, scary as hell and sad, too."

"So, you closed the lids?" Joe knew it was a natural impulse to close a dead man's eyes.

"No, not me." He was obviously shaken. "When I came back after calling 911, the eyes on both of 'em, they were closed. But I swear, I didn't touch them. Mick's yelled at me enough to not touch no bodies. It was the little one of the two women. She came back, rushed off with her purse slung over her shoulder."

"The little one? Then you're saying it was a pair of women with the men when they entered?"

"Talked to the cabbie that brought the foursome here; got no idea how he fit four adults in that rickshaw of his."

"Canopied three-wheeler, peddle propelled job?" Mick wanted to light up a cigarette, but Joe gave him the Coran stare, and it worked. Mick kept the unlit Camel in his mouth.

"Yeah, you know, 'bout to fall apart. Terry stopped long enough to get cigarettes outta the machine in the lobby."

"You mean you know this guy?" Joe felt a moment's sense of finding a firm connection in this chaos.

"Sure, comes around regular...same like tonight. Makes shit money. Same like me, so we talk."

"Do you know the girls who used the room?"

"They signed for the room, Catherine and Tammy, said they were cousins, but they change all the time like I'm some idiot who could care."

"So, you think you could pick them out in a lineup?" Joe's eyes stayed on Norm.

"Sure, sure if there's cash in it."

"No cash, Norm," Mick assured him. "Just the knowledge of doing your civic duty.

"Alright, but I can't lose time from the job, so if it's during daylight hours, and I guess OK." He then added. "Well, I'll leave all this to you fellas." He handed the key back to Mick. "Just lock up and return the key to the desk when you're done." Norm started out but stopped sort of doing so, saying, "Oh yeah, Mick, I got this for ya." Norm held his iPhone up for Mick to see a blurry photo of the back of a thin woman hitting the bricks, rushing from the hotel. "It's the little one."

Mick gave the night man a guffaw. "Doesn't help any more than the fake license plate and name you took from the 'big' one, Norm. Still, send the photo to my phone. You still got me as a friend, right, Norm?" Mick asked, shuffling the key on its chain.

Norm assured him of their internet connection and left.

Mick then found Lawler bending over the body of the man on the left side. "What're you up to, Columbo? Opening the eyelids, putting them back to how Norm said they were?"

"Curious why the one prostitute closed the eyelids. Either freaked her out, staring at her, you know like in Poe's *Tell-Tale Heart*, or…"

"Or?"

"…or the little one, she has some pint of compassion, empathy, you know. Maybe even regret at what's happened to these two poor bastards. So, she closes the eyelids in a show of remorse…*maybe*?"

"If so, a little late for remorse."

"Same kinda regret that had someone taping two lovers' hands together in death…*maybe*?"

"Is that all you've got, Columbo?"

"Getting annoying Mick, calling me that."

"Prefer Poirot or Sherlock?"

"First thing I want the coroner's man to take DNA on the one set of eyes and prints on the other set of eyes."

"And then?"

"*Petechial* hemorrhaging in the eyes—proof of strangulation."

Mick, unbeknownst to Joe, had lifted the hand of the man on the right side of the bed, and he held it up, not for a shake or a high five, but to show a heavy handcuff dangling from the dead man's hand. Mick rattled the cuffs for Joe, and even in the poor light, Lawler saw the evidence that the deceased had been handcuffed with the real thing.

Once again Loudin was the Coroner's Investigator assigned to this scene of death. "You two lost? Kind of a long way from Stewart, aren't you?" she wondered aloud.

With a wry smile, Joe changed the subject, asking, "Appears you've already won your degree in Dr. Coran's class."

"My second go-round, so I already had built up points."

"So, I won't have a partner on the special assignment case the doc handed us, *eh*?"

"I'd be happy to consult on it, Joe. No reason I can't help you out."

She reminded Joe of Perkins. Lawler gave her a rare smile and said, "You'd do that for me?"

"Come on, Joe. I'd do that for anyone I had partnered up with. Wouldn't you, Joe?"

"Just meant to say…thanks."

"Going to miss me in class, aren't you?"

"I am, yes."

"This way though, you can buy me dinner."

A quasi date, he thought. "Sure, it's a date." He took notice that she didn't cringe at the word *date*.

Mick stood at a respectful distance and hadn't interrupted or barged into their conversation, which had Lawler wondering if his police partner was fighting off some internal issues or personal concerns haunting him at the moment. Maybe financial woes. It'd become clear to Joe that many a cop in this town had become gambling addicts. The allure faced people at every turn.

"Before your guys take the two dead guys out, Katheine, would you indulge me?"

"What is it?"

"If you would, take DNA off the eyelids and maybe prints as well. I mean maybe best to do the prints on one set of eyelids, DNA on the other guy's lids. We have reason to believe that one of the killers closed the eyes."

"Ha, is that right? And you're sure of this?"

"Night man witnessed enough to give us the clue, yes."

"Will do then. No Biggy."

"She dug into her black bag for the swab kit and the print kit and went to work. "Just how did you surmise murder here, Joe?"

"Cuffs—the real kind," he said, holding the one up with a pencil, and I suspect a sexy silk necktie for a second thing. Had a quick look-see, petechial hemorrhaging in the one's eyes."

"I ought to report you to Dr. T."

"But you won't," said Mick, standing beside Lawler now.

Frowning, she agreed. "But I won't. This time…"

TWENTY-ONE

Days later

Mick, checking with his many connections – casino musclemen, dealers, show girls, waitresses, bar girls and men, buskers working Fremont, cabbies and three-wheelers, even a pimp he used as a snitch, was getting less than nowhere, until he struck gold at the *Golden Nugget*. Of course, he had Norman the night man on notice to contact him immediately should the 'rickshaw' man show up at the hotel again, the man who'd brought the Cat and Tammy to the hotel.

The luck at the *Golden Nugget* hit when Mick flashed the poor photo of the walking away, back to the camera woman that Norm had caught while thinking the two women had had a tiff, and that they meant to stiff him on their bill, thus the rushed photo. The two red costumed showgirls who, on first glimpse, shook their heads and with one laughingly saying, "That's rich, Officer Mick, a woman's back. Sure, looks familiar, it does."

Mick had thanked them and had started away, when the other said, "Hold on! Let me see that *backside* again."

Mick pulled the picture up on his iPhone again. "That cute little shoulder purse," began Marilee, I think it's the same one the little thing had with her when she and that bitch Cat had with her on Fremont, wouldn't move for our time the other night. Think she called her Harley, but I just remember that studded purse. Like something you see in a biker."

Mick wondered if the showgirl was just swatting some girl she had a grudge against. Still, he asked the other tall partner, "Did you notice the purse, and does it look the same in the photo?"

"Sure does, now that Tawney pointed it out."

"You guys seem anxious to get me after this lady."

"Not just her," one said.

"Cat too," the other assured him.

"Cat's a real bitch of the first order."

"Other one was just trying to please Cat."

Mick had expended a lot of time and effort on finding pairs who worked men together. Not surprising in these days of violence against women, there proved to be many pairs plying their trade this way in Vegas, but Norm at some point recalled the sound of a whip inside the death trap. He'd called Mick with the information. Not all the pairs used a whip. And these two showgirls were bent on bringing on trouble to this Cat, adding that a whip was part of her dominatrix avatar on Fremont Street. Swatting her perhaps, a new and common enough practice.

"Wouldn't be hard to stake her out," said Marilee, between picking her teeth.

"She's a *busker*," added Tawney. "Sets up like she's some tough bitch, which she is!" Both ladies broke into laughter at this. "No better than a lowlife streetwalker."

"Smart cop like you, Mick…bet you can cuff her and show she isn't so tough after all."

"You girls, why do you hate this Cat lady so much?"

"She treated us other night like we didn't matter," replied Tawny.

"And they go too far with the groping and sleazy posing. Makes us all look trashy added Marilee. "Almost turned them *inta* Fremont Street Association."

"But that's not done 'mong respectable ladies. Still, the two of 'em ran over on our time!"

"Wouldn't be hard to stake her out," Marille said for a second time over the noise of the casino.

"She's a buk-ster," added Tawney.

"Penny-pitching munching buskers is all." Mick knew the term, and it appeared that this Lady Cat, Harley, the showgirls, all posers and performers worked the street for tips.

"Smart cop like you, Mick…bet you can cuff her and show she isn't so tough after all."

"You girls, why do you hate this Cat lady so much?"

"She treated us other night like we didn't matter," replied Arleen.

"Ran overtime and took some of our time," repeated Tawney.

"You sure it's the same purse in the photo then?"

"What're ya deaf? If Tawney says its it, then it's it." Arleen shrugged, while Tawney said, "Absolutely one hundred percent."

"You think the two of them might be on Fremont tonight?"

"That's what they do!"

You sayin' that's all they do?"

"Aside hustling *old man tourists*, yeah."

"Too ugly to do what we do!"

The following night

Mick and Joe continued in their walking stakeout, watching for the two women that'd been described to them. After a while Joe was ready to give up the ghost, saying, "These grifters could be in Texas for all we know, living large on credit card fished off dead men."

They again wore plainclothes about Fremont in a casual and touristy way eyes bulging at the many shows put on here, keeping an eye out for the two ladies they now knew as Lady Cat and Harley. The only two names that their sources had given them. It didn't take long for them to hear the crack of Lady C's whip and to see the dominatrix outfitted, tall lady and beside her a shy looking smaller woman whose shyness appeared part of the act as Lady C dominated Harley, making her crawl and lick the Cat's boots and work her way upward along her master's legs and see-through mesh stockings, up and up to the sweet spot, covered in panty-like shorts.

"*What'daya* think, Joe? We take them in for questioning here and now, before the crowd and risk a protest, or we introduce ourselves as a couple of interested Johns who know George Washington?"

"See where that leads us?"

"Why not. Just don't allow any handcuff play.'

"Orrrrr harnesses."

Mick and Joe gave the busking ladies a look over to let them know the men were definitely interested. Then Mick flashed a hundred-dollar bill, saying, "More where that comes from" before he tucked the bill away. Joe dropped a twenty in the Cat's collection box."

"Just in time," Cat said. "Our time's up."

Both Mick and Joe noticed the smaller lady, childlike in her mannerism and appearance had the tell-tale black studded purse strapped over her shoulder now, preparing to leave. "I'm tired, Cat," she muttered as if exhausted, sighing heavily.

Part of her play acting or an authentic sigh, Lawler wondered.

"Wave down a cab for us, big guy," Cat ordered Mick.

"You mean a pedicab?" Mick replied.

"No, a cab-cab, and you're paying."

"Where're we going? To the desert for starlight?"

"Better than that," Cat said, rolling her whip up and placing it in a guitar-sized suitcase.

Harley bitched, "My feet and knees are killing me."

"Get that cab, fatty," Cat again ordered Mick, who said, "My name, *honeybunch*, is George, and my business partner here is Jake."

"You sure it's the same purse in the photo, Mick?" Lawler whispered?"

"*Whataya* think, Joe? We take them in for questioning here and now, in front of the crowd and risk a protest, or we introduce ourselves as a couple of interested Johns who know George Washington?"

"See where that leads us? Why not? But again, I say no handcuff play unless the cuffs are ours and on these two."

"*Orrrrr* harnesses," restated Mick.

139

Again, the little woman began licking the larger one's boots. "*Part of her role or an authentic sense of worthlessness*, Lawler wondered.

"Wave down a cab for us, big guy," Cat *ordered* Mick again, and Mick repeated himself as if mocking the woman, saying, "You mean a pedicab, right?"

"No, damn you! A fuckin' cab-cab, and you're paying."

"Where we going?" Mick insisted on knowing.

"Better than you might imagine, big boy," Cat said, while still working to fit her whip into her suitcase.

Harley continued to bitch. "My feet and knees really are killing me, Cat."

"Get that cab, fatty," Cat again ordered Mick, who said,

"My name, honey babe, is George, and my business partner here is Jake."

"Well tell Jake to get us a cab!"

"Destination first, 'George' demanded.

"I see you're going to need a good whippin', George." Look, our destination's a big surprise. One you'll love, deary. Isn't that right, Tammy?"

"Yeah, anybody'd love it. First thing I need is a hot bath."

Neither Joe nor Mick knew what the two were talking about. Joe hailed a city cab down. The two ladies climbed in back with Mick, while Joe found the upfront co-pilot seat, disregarding the cabbie's protest that no one sat upfront. Once the heavyset amiable cab driver realized that Joe wasn't moving and given Cat's suitcase there really was no room in the rear for Joe, he began talking of the day's news, his kids, a recent film he'd watched, and staring in his rearview mirror, seeing that Mick was being felt up by the two women, he asked, "Where to?"

Cat shouted, "The Palace!"

"Really?" both driver and Mick blurted in unison.

"So that's the big surprise?" Joe chimed in.

"We're not your usual girls, are we, Tammy?"

"No. No we're not," Harley replied in a mouse's squeak, and Joe wondered if Tammy had perhaps felt the sting of the cat whip.

"Wow," Mick added. "The Palace! You do the cloak room?"

"Hell no! We got our own private room and room service."

The cab driver whistled and said to Joe, "You boys better be going in careful."

Joe was unsure what kind of careful the man meant, but he could think of four or five interpretations with Lady Cat and Harley.

The cab pulled into the covered entryway to the Palace, and while the others piled out, he paid the driver, showed him his shoulder holster and badge, saying, "You don't have to worry about me and Mick, my friend. We're on a case, and these ladies are possible witnesses."

"I'll be damned. Something to tell Lily and the boys about."

Joe made his way from the cab, joining the party and gentlemanly taking the suitcase from Cat to which she smiled, and surprised, she said, "Why, thank you. Aren't you sweet."

"Well…a lady should have a man carry for her."

"Like those pictures in *National Geographic* of women alone carrying pots of water on their heads," Mick added.

At the same time, Cat said to Tammy, "Jake called me a lady, Tam…*a lady*."

The party rushed by the registry and into an elevator. They were soon on the 8th floor, going down the hallway to the private room, Cat saying, Tammy, Jake is mine. You can have George."

As Cat spoke, both Mick and Joe noted the room number: **813** and going through their heads was the obvious. Had this room been let out to two dead men found by Norman at that seedy old motel in the back alleyway behind Fremont, two men still without names in the morgue? The dead tourists' room, that is before they were murdered.

Why wouldn't a brazen pair of women like Cat and Harley take the murdered men's Palace card keys?

TWENTY-TWO

411-01: shortly arrest imminent.

Once inside the immaculate room, the only sign anyone had ever been in the room at all, a pair of slippers and two plush white robes indicating His and Hers, as usual, lying across the bed, a few items of clothing draped over a corner chair, a number of tiny alcohol bottles robbed from the mini bar. Otherwise, the ladies had maintained a well-kept room, but of course most of it likely fell on the room service.

Lady C as she billed herself waste no time, as if in a rush to be done with the men and the night, so she snatched away the heavy, fluffy white Afghan cover and growled in lioness style, ordering Harley to strip down and "on the bed sheets, *sweetums* and do your little-poor-thing whining and whimpering like the little pussy cat you are, or else, you know I'll beat you blue down there…hehehe!"

"But I *wanna* bath first, my Lady Lord."

"Forget that! Men like a dirty, filthy thing just like you are. You want her dirty, right George?"

"*Ahhh*, either way's fine, but she wants a shower, I could climb in with her."

"Fantasy of yours, Fat Boy?" Lady C had found her whip and cracked it near Mick's arm. "Alright, go for it.

Jake and me, we'll have our fun here. Go! Enjoy Harley if you can wake her ass up!"

With Mick heading for the shower along with Harley, Joe's blue sense kicked in, and it told him that Mick meant to separate the two suspects. Of course, showering with Harley butt naked had nothing to do with it.

Now Joe was alone with the boss of this traveling, possibly deadly duo, and Lady C wasted no time with the tease play, grinding for 'Jake', and about the time Joe heard the shower turn on and a loud slap—likely to Harley's backside, the cat purred and went to her knees over her box of toys and instruments of 'pleasure' which included handcuffs, electric shock items, huge dildos, and tightly folded harnesses, as well as silken scarves, feathered toys and nipple clamps. There seemed a veritable X-rated store inside her case.

She ordered Joe, "Remove your clothes and lay down! Face down on the bed, and if you don't do as I say, you'll get the beating of your life!" She cracked the little half-whip for punctuation. "I know your secret desire for humiliation, and that's why you picked me of all the women you saw on Fremont! Right baby?"

"I just want normal…simple…easy sex, Lady C. No beating with a whip!"

"Alright, fine, but you *gotta* at least let me handcuff you, sweety. I do my best work on a helpless man. You'll like it that way, too!"

"No, not unless we use *my* cuffs on *you* kitty cat," he replied, holding up his set.

Lady C gasped in horror, turned and rushed toward the restroom, shouting Harley's name, but the cat lady didn't get far, as Joe clipped her, using his knee as in training to send her knee into a crippling circumstance, sending her straight on her face, bruising nose and mouth. At the same time, he wondered if they really had the right pair here, the old-man-tourists killers. And while cuffing Lady C, he realized that Mick was still cavorting with Harley in the shower and had likely heard nothing of the scuffle.

With the wildcat subdued, Lawler entered the bathroom, found a towel and Mick's cuffs below his discarded pants, and tore back the shower curtain, ordering Mick to cuff the girl while he toweled her down. "We're taking them to Stewart for processing. Get dressed and do what you can to get her dressed."

"Where's the cat lady?" asked Mick.

"Cuffed, face down on the floor. Ten to one those last two dead guys booked this room, and we can find out easy enough at the desk."

The two cops, unofficially working undercover, doing decoy work, *slowed down* to first take the suspect ladies to the desk, where they gathered information on *who* had actually booked 813. The answer was a nail in the coffin for Maureen and Harley, as the keys to room 813 was *definitely* not theirs, and yet they had possession of the card keys.

Under questioning, the interrogation with Cat returned no results except to realize the depth of her stubbornness and her hatred of men. It went deep as the roots of an oak. Neither Mick nor Joe had gotten '*anywhere but nowhere*' as Mick had put it to him on coming out of the interrogation with Lady C, who was given to screeching and spitting like a real cat. Was the big woman delusional or building fodder for a case for mental instability? Mick and Lawler kicked it over before Chief Lewis rushed in, angry, having learned of what was going on this late night in his stationhouse without his knowledge. He'd also, according to Daisy been pulled away from his weekly poker game with his cadre of friends.

"*He's got friends?*" Joe said it before Mick could get it out, and both laughed.

Mick tried to cut the Chief off before he could get to Lawler, sure that Joe would be Lewis' prime target. "We think we have a pair of hookers turned murderers, Chief, and if so, this case, well it's going to go national…put our department and Stewart on the map, maybe even *Inside Edition* or *20/20* or 48 *Hours*, although it's taken more than—"

"Shut the hell up. Mick. Just *outta* my way. I'm talking to Lawler on this. Sherlock, I should say!"

Joe met his Chief halfway. "Mick's right, Chief. These two women have been victimizing tourists possibly for years, we don't know how many tourists they've killed. We have to break the younger one, so we put Duk in there with her. The other one has given nothing up. But we're…we have good reason for hope, sir."

"*Hmmm…*" muttered Lewis, pulling at his chin hair. "So, Mick, you know any TV connections? I mean 48 Hours is damned big stuff. You think Duk can break the other one?"

"She's falling apart already, Cap. In no time, and as the guys with the cameras, I know a few, sure."

"I'm sure of breaking the other one down as a possible accomplice," began Lawler, and if so, we'll be saving future victims."

Daisy was going off shift, but instead of leaving, she joined the three men on the viewing side of the one-way interrogation room window, where they turned on the mic to hear how it was going between Harley and Duk. The fragile Harley wanted to go back home to Indiana, she pleaded, fast falling apart out of fear of Cat. "She could turn on me and kill me anytime! She's a *schizoid*, but I'm not like her. I ain't for killing nobody."

***

With evidence collected by Katherine Loudin via DNA swabs, and with help from Dr. Coran, the DNA from the eyelids and fingerprints, the interrogation with Tammy quickly turned from interrogation to 'hands up, you got me'. After all, they also had her DNA on the classroom tape. Once the law made it clear to Tammy that they knew Maureen 'ran' the murders, Tammy broke into tears and shaking sobs. The next step was simple,

Lawler thought: *Play on Tammy Harley's good heart and flip her.*

The four murders and perhaps more marked Cat as a female serial killer reminiscent of Florida's Eileen Wuornos, whose victims were mostly elderly men, lonely and *looking for love in all the wrong places*, as the song went.

Once the case against the women appeared a tight sure deal, Mick the following day put Lawler into a head lock and said, "Hey lawman Lawler, I want to thank you— Joey!

Joe pulled loose. "Thanks for what, Mick?"

"Reminding me that the work of a lawman is honorable, and that honor's hard won. You brought that back to me, even here in this dishonorable haven of corruption and—"

"Come on, Mick, you're going to get me blushing, and I don't blush."

TWENTY-THREE

410-2: Secure, all's well.

In class, Dr Coran surprised Lawler, using him as an example of what *can* be done at a crime scene, saying, "If one keeps an open mind and does not shut down on the circumstances that, on the surface alone told one story, when in fact a killer set the stage for misinterpretation." Coran went back to the first moments that Joe had had suspicions when others took a murder scene as a double suicide. It proved to in fact be a double murder." She held up the tape—or rather a ball of classroom display, as the original tape was now certain evidence in the new case against Maureen and Tammy.

"Joe had enough imagination to see what proved to be invisible to everyone else in the room that night, which led him and his partner to a separate suspicion beyond the belief of others, including the coroner's man." She continued to tell the class where Joe's open mind and imagination had led, about the eyelid DNA and prints lifted from the two victims of murder in the more recent case.

Dr. Coran then began applauding for Joe, and the whole class joined in. She then began praising and applause for Katherin Loudin for her help in the lab beside the professor, matching the DNA from the eyelids to that on the tape used in the classroom assignment. "The free dinner for two goes to Joe and Kathi."

This announcement, ending any attempt for others to win a dinner at the top of the Space Needle's 360-degree revolving restaurant, atop the newly branded Stratosphere to the *STRAT,* slowly ended any further cheers or clapping. Now, only muttered congratulations of an off-handed nature slow-walked the room. To reward her other students, Dr. Jessica Coran called an early dismissal.

***

In the Rattler and heading for Stewart PD, Joe somehow heard the familiar crackling of his radio over the rattling. He expected to hear Daisy with some domestic or disorderly call, but no, it was Mick on the radio saying, "Buddy, you gotta get your behind to the station here and now. Chief wants to see us together…on the double."

"Hell, on my way there now, Mick!"

Over the radio on a more secure frequency, Mick said, "Maybe you oughta go for detective, pal, Columbo. Take the test."

"Nah, tried that in Illinois and just got hammered for trying."

"Hammered by the dicks?"

"No, all my uniformed buddies…didn't like me after that, even after I failed the test, and I think the dicks didn't want me to succeed either. Think the test was rigged against me. Looked like it was AI rigged. Of course, that's crap, but something seemed off."

"Damn...I was thinking you had it easier back there in good old Ill-in-noise."

"There ain't no noise in Illinois—*naw* is all, French, I think. Or French and Indian."

"Just get here, fast!"

***

When Lawler pulled into the underground lot, windows open, the Rattler's astounding noise was only amplified, so much so that the carpool guys covered their ears. "When the hell is Mick going to fix this damn problem," he said to himself, quick to park and shut down. He took the elevator to the main floor and opened on everyone in the department, even Detective Duk, clapping and cheering, a poor sad bunch of balloons waving and Daisy pointing to a quickly decorated folding table with a cake atop it.

"Whoa, folks, it's not my birthday. Somebody's got it wrong!" His accusing eyes fixed on Daisy.

"This is for corralling those two serial killer bitches," said Chief Gabe Lewis, reaching out, shaking Joe's hand, Joe quick to say, I didn't do that alone! I had Mick's help, and without Mick's training and guidance, well...we'd've surely lost the killers. Tammy Harley *said* they were packing, leaving Vegas for Los Angeles."

"Yeah, for better 'pickings', she said, added Detective Duk."

Mick shouted, "Partner, no need being modest. In the end, it was all your instincts that got Cat and Harley."

"Let's all dig into that cake I baked," Daisy shouted, and soon the three-layer cake was being cut with their deft handling of a huge kitchen knife, everyone standing clear of the blade.

Dr. Coran stepped from behind the crowd and said, "Daisy, I could use that knife in my autopsy room."

Loudin, smiling, added, "I believe that!"

This got a laugh from everyone, even Duk and Chief Lewis.

EPILOGUE

Code 400-0: Unofficial: Dating is murder…

Lawler pulled in front of the address Loudin had given him. It was a typical small southern Nevada lot in Henderson, a stucco covered geodesic dome home. Rare but not unheard of. The east side showed lots of windows and a patio door to the front. The rest of the dome on the west side had smaller shuttered and curtained windows. The front yard was taken up by a large semi-circular driveway with more than enough parking space. The backyard was obscured by green and pink shrubbery, forming a hedge fence.

Lawler texted Loudin: *I am here*. While texting, he walked up to the front patio doors. She met him at the doors and looked to where he had parked his electric Harley Davidson motorcycle.

"You've gotta be kidding? Didn't I tell you I couldn't take one of those air tours over the city or Grand Canyon because I get air sick? And so, you expect me to go out in my best gown on the back of that thing?" She pointed. "You couldn't even spring for a Lyft or an Uber?"

"*Heyyy*, I thought it'd be fun, and I could take you out to some of my favorite roads and trailways through the mountains."

"Let's just stick to dinner. We'll take my car."

"Great, I'll drive," said Lawler.

"No, you won't. I am driving my own car. One moment, while I get the keys."

 Lawler followed her inside and was surprised to see that the front room was basically a small sitting room with a conversation pit seating arrangement. He wondered about a door with a fingerprint-keypad lock. Keeping up with her down a hallway that he tried to follow her into, muttering small talk, wishing to continue the conversation.

She abruptly stopped, turning with an upraised hand, saying, "Woah there, Chief cowboy. I don't know you well enough for *back-hall* privileges just yet. Have a seat in the front room, until I get back."

"What is this? The feminist version of Blue Beard's castle?"

"Something like that, yes."

Lawler whistled. "I guess you have depths I hadn't seen before now, Kathi," he half joked.

"You don't know the half of it."

"Well, I'd like to."

"Give it time. Let's start with dinner."

Loudin set the house alarm, and locked the door behind them, and they got into her lime green convertible PT cruiser, found under an attached carport.

"Where to?" Loudin asked, then shouted, "Hey!" when Lawler snatched her phone and put an address into the map program. He put it back into the cupholder where she could glance down at the map, and they could both hear the AI voice verbal instructions.

"You could have just said the stratosphere. It's easy to get to. You can see it from anywhere in the valley and it's like having a magnetic north compass to navigate by. Stratosphere North. Luxor pyramids sky beam South."

They parked in self-parking. Went through the casino's clanging slot machines and up the escalators to the mezzanine shopping mall area. From there they went through security, and up the elevator for the 800 feet ride to the 106th floor. Once there, the elevator doors opened on the flashy, bright top of the world rotating restaurant that gave a 360°-degree view of the Vegas Valley. From the fabulous Las Vegas strip to glitter Gulch downtown on Fremont Street to the suburbs with the orange slate rooftops and tan stucco siding. All this plus the parks, waters, and mountains that surround the city on all sides.

Loudin complained anyway, saying, "I can't believe we had to go through security to go up the elevators."

"Yeah, it's a holdover from the heightened security after the 911 bombings."

With that said, they were seated by a hostess looking like a model from a Gucci advertisement.

Dusk over Vegas from the perspective of near a hundred feet up in a revolving restaurant proved amazing for the sights, not so much as the wild circus city lights as the sprawling valley and the mountains encircling Vegas on all sides. Lawler felt a calm he'd not felt here in his new home that seemed foreign, and it was surely the wine and sitting across from Katherine as much as the semi-darkness of the lavish restaurant and having it move under his feet. The sights below might account for a good part of the high overtaking him when a sudden admission from Loudin sent all his quiet self-searching into some other realm.

"I've wanted to be alone with you, Joe, since that first day you came into our classroom--late, of course."

"Not that late; maybe five minutes. Didn't know the room number."

"Joe, you began the class a month behind everyone else!"

"Oh, yeah, but not a month. Three weeks only. The instructor for 101 had a stroke and suddenly…well they couldn't find anyone else to take over for Dr. Wayne."

"Lucky…I mean sad for the old prof, but lucky for our class that you came. We all learned almost as much from you as we did from Dr. Coran."

"That's going way too far, Kathi."

She had told him to call her Kathi. "I don't think so, Joseph Lawler."

"I remember that first day in Coran's class too."

"You do? What do you remember, Joe?"

"You shot me a smile when no one else in the room bothered to look up."

"We'd been ordered by Teach to concentrate on reading her syllabus, because some of the students obviously hadn't bothered."

They continued their pleasant small talk that turned to their admiration of one another, and she surprised him, coming around the table to it sit in his lap showgirl fashion, kicking her leg into the air and getting stares from other patrons. More than one patron called out, "I'll have what he's having."

Joe grew somewhat red-cheeked, so she kissed him. "That clear enough, Officer? Or do you need a full-on Lauren Bacall line? Just whistle…you know how to whistle, don't you?"

He did his best Bogart imitation, replying, "Kathi, I think this may be the beginning of long and fruitful binary relationship."

The End – but only *of book one…Author bios below:*

Author Biographies

Brief Autobiography - Gene E. Kelly:

I am a veteran of USMC JAG (Judge Advocate General's Office), County Forest Rangers, have worked as a beat cop, Death Investigator, Chief of Police, and as Department Head for private sector Corporate Security. Summary at:
https://www.kellylasvegas.com/consult/index.html

As a work of fiction, The **Blue Vegas novella series** is inspired by tall tales and police stories often imparted over coffee or while chatting car to car. As well as a blend of Midwest, west coast, TV and movie procedures that have become part of LEO (Law Enforcement Officer) myth and lore over the years.

I have enjoyed working background and as a LEO consultant for books and movies over the years. It has been a long time since I have been on a shift, meaning that technology, equipment, case law and procedures have changed many times over since "back in the day." In addition, many of the elements and incidents of this story, while outright and complete fiction, are also based on police lore past, and a possible alternate police path of the future. All of the characters, incidents, and some of the locations are works of fiction, and any resemblance to any persons, living, dead, or undead, are complete coincidence.

I cannot stress enough how much Robert W. Walker's research and extensive career accomplishments in the field of police thrillers have ultimately shaped and formed this novella and the following sequels and possible prequels.

– Gene E. Kelly, March 2024, Las Vegas, Nevada.

Brief Autobiography – Robert W. Walker:

I have devoted my life to two obsessions—writing (working toward a new goal now of a hundred books) and to teaching (the honorable profession). I concentrated on the art of writing, despite the beliefs of so many that it is a born talent and cannot be taught. There are many, many skills in the art of writing, as is the case with any art, that can be learned, and all artists in all fields study the masters and the classics. Certainly, growing up in inner-city Chicago, one either goes into crime, politics, or writing about the other two. Much of my learning to write was studying how the masters used their tools to have readers laugh, cry, sympathize with make-believe people and sometimes animals or even ghosts.

As a high school student, I fell in love with Mark Twain's boys books, Tom and Huck, and learning my hero wrote no sequel, I wrote it for him, and the early novel, *Daniel Webster Jackson & the Wrongway Railroad* won me a full-ride scholarship out of Chicago and into Northwestern University, where I got my grounding in the art of teaching. Another art that people can learn by studying the masters, and by learning how to use the proper tools and skills for the job. Imagine garnering a scholarship at a major university not for basketball or football but for writing. Out of it all, like Twain, my spiritual mentor, I wished to be as versatile an author as he, and as good a teacher as he. I suspect that his *Prince & the Pauper* was his way of again working with Tom & Huck.

See my class in a book *Dead on Writing, the how-to for the dysfunctional writer in us all.*

– Robert W. Walker, March 2024, WV

https://robertwalkerbooks.com/

124dd002-964e-42e3-86a7-f6adcdc791caR01